Hope For Joshua

Renée Vajko Srch

Published by Pen It! Publications, LLC
812-371-4128   www.penitpublications.com

ISBN: 978-1-952011-75-7
Edited by Anna Garrison Nemeth
Cover Design by Donna Cook

Contents

DEDICATION

To my husband, Len.

Your love and support made this book possible.

CHAPTER ONE

When Mother told me parenthood would alter my life, I'd shrugged it off as sentimental banter. Back then, life seemed so simple. I'd assumed parenting would be a breeze. Looking back, I wonder at the confidence and eagerness with which I'd embraced each new day.

Four years later, I find myself wishing I could recapture some of that youthful enthusiasm. I could use a strong dose of optimism right about now. It's only eight in the morning and I'm already exhausted. Although it's been a long time since I've slept through the night, this is more than ordinary fatigue. It's a muddle of tiredness, melancholy, discouragement, and pure weariness, which drags at every bone and every sinew of my being.

"Would you like to watch the weather while I get dressed?" I ask Joshua, pushing myself away from the table.

A few stray Cheerios under his chair catch my eye. As I bend to retrieve them, long strands of flaxen hair tumble over my shoulders. I cringe, noticing how dull and dried out it looks. I really should schedule a visit to Doo or Dye Hair Salon, but just don't have time for that particular luxury right now.

My thoughts turn to the bottle of Tangerine Blast hair dye stashed in the cabinet under my bathroom sink. Perhaps I can indulge in a few highlights while my four-year old watches TV.

Silently, Joshua slides off the kitchen chair and pads into the living-room, switching on the Weather Channel with the remote.

"….elevated temperatures continue throughout southwest Missouri as a warm front pushes through…," drawls the meteorologist. It's only June, but heat warnings are already being issued for Springfield and the surrounding areas.

Clapping his hands, Joshua twirls around and around as the forecaster traces invisible weather fronts with her hands like a meteorological maestro. He's in his happy place where heatwaves and storm fronts are cause for celebration.

"If you need something, Mommy will be upstairs, okay?" I say, attempting to make eye contact. But he's in a world of his own, one to which I'm not privy. Oblivious, Joshua weaves and waves like the inflatable Tube Man at the Ford dealership.

Wishing I had half his energy, I return to the kitchen, pour myself another cup of coffee, then drag myself upstairs. Cradling my mug in both hands, I savor the heady aroma of home-brewed Arabica and wonder when the caffeine will kick in. There was a time when two cupfuls rendered me as hyper as a kid with a sugar rush. Today, I'm on my third, yet I'm still feeling sluggish.

This should be quick and simple, I think, reading the instructions on the hair dye. It appears fairly easy to apply and doesn't require as much time to set as some of the other dyes I've tried. As I set my mug on the shelf over the sink, the words *'BEST MOM'* catch my eye. The large, bold letters printed on the side of the cup seem to taunt and tease. What was intended as a thoughtful Mother's Day gift merely reminds me how many times I've botched up.

After opening the bottle of Tangerine Blast, I slip on the nitrile gloves, then start brushing the copper-colored dye through several locks on the left side of my scalp. I'm experimenting with a new dyeing technique called *balayage*. According to an article in *Beauty Today*, it's supposed to deliver a more natural, sun-kissed appearance. To be honest, I look like I've stuck my head up a rusty drainpipe.

A loud *bang* makes me jump. The bottle slips from my hand and shatters. Like a river of molten lava, flaming-orange dye flows into the sink.

"Oh, shucks" I groan, yanking off the nitrile gloves. Tossing them into the sink, I rush downstairs.

"Joshua!" I call, glancing into the living-room.

The television is on, but Joshua is no longer around. Snatching up the remote, I kill the sound.

"Joshua!"

I pause. Wait. Listen.

The house is unnervingly quiet.

"Joshua!" I call, over and over, as I check the kitchen, the dining-room, the guest bathroom. He's not downstairs.

Sprinting back up the stairs, I open his bedroom door, praying I'll find him playing with his toys or lying on his bed. But his room is empty. A flicker of fear sparks in my heart. Dropping to my knees, I search under the bed. Nothing but a balled-up sock and a broken blue crayon.

I check the tight space between his wooden dresser and bookcase, where Joshua sometimes wedges himself when he's anxious or upset, but he's not there.

"Joshua! Where are you, Joshua?" My voice trembles as I call his name over and over. If anything has happened to my little boy –.

My heart clenches as the chilling screech of brakes rips through the stillness of a suburban workday morning. I can taste fear at the back of my throat.

"Please don't let that be my baby," I moan.

For an endless second, I'm frozen to the spot. I can't move. I can't think. Fear holds me prisoner. An image of my little boy, lying in a heap on the hard asphalt, his tiny body twisted at odd angles, leaps to mind. The thought wrenches a groan from deep within me.

The blare of a horn and a stream of obscenities wake me from my stupor, releasing me from fear's cloying grip. Pounding down the stairs, I wrench open the front door and take the porch steps two at a time. Sprinting down the drive, I reach the road just in time to spot two taillights disappearing around the corner. The street is deserted, save for a black cat cowering behind our neighbor's grey Ford pickup. It glances at me with big, round eyes before dashing away.

"Thank you, God," I whisper, sagging against the truck.

The adrenaline rush leaves me shaken and unsteady. Somehow, I manage to stagger up the drive and into the house. As I turn the lock, it suddenly dawns on me; I never disengaged the bolt when I ran outside. *Did I forget to lock it after Martin left for work?* I wonder. *Worse yet, has Joshua figured out how to operate the deadbolt?*

My mind races through this morning's events, but they're mostly a blur. Burying my face in my hands, I try to recall my actions after Martin yelled out a hasty "goodbye." Did I turn the lock, or didn't I? It's no use. My recollections are as elusive as those stuffed toys in a claw machine. Just as I think I've latched onto something, it slips away.

Regardless, I need to face the inevitable truth; Joshua is missing.

CHAPTER TWO

It only takes a couple of minutes to scan the driveway and the tiny square of lawn claiming to be our front yard. Dry grass crunches underfoot as my slippered feet tromp across the lawn to check the narrow space between our house and the neighbors'. The frivolous gap yields nothing other than yellowing grass and the wooden privacy fence which delineates our properties.

The fact that I'm wearing my *Hello Kitty* summer pajamas outside is the least of my worries. I'm only concerned about finding Joshua. My mind runs the gamut of frightening scenarios. For all I know, he could be in real danger. The thought triggers a rush of tears. I swipe at them, impatient with myself. This is not the time to fall apart.

Sadly, this is not Joshua's first incident. Two months ago, he wandered out of the house, leaving the front door open behind him. After searching up and down our cul-de-sac, my husband and I were about to call the police when the Johnsons, our neighbors two doors down, discovered him in their back yard, playing with their beagle.

The second time he disappeared, our neighbor Clara found him wandering down the street. She'd grabbed his hand and hauled him home, kicking and screaming. That second incident drove us to install a deadbolt on the front door to supplement the knob lock. Yet here I am again, searching for my son.

Struggling to see through the tears, I scurry up Sycamore Street. I glance left and right, wiping beads of sweat from my top lip. The taupe cookie-cutter houses, erected seemingly overnight, look so similar, it could be confusing to a lost child trying to find his way home.

Guilt swells over me like a tidal wave. Guilt for leaving Joshua unsupervised, guilt for messing with my hair while my son watched TV. To be candid, I've been craving some me-time; a little self-pampering, a small taste of normalcy in a home that is far from ordinary. Is that so awful? Apparently so, because now I'm paying for my selfish behavior.

Venturing into the Wilsons' backyard, I approach their large, above-ground pool. My legs are as wobbly as a newborn calf's as I struggle to quell the fear inside.

"Oh, God, no!" I scream, as I notice something round and yellow bobbing up and down.

10

Breaking into a run, I reach the pool and lean over the side. I stagger backwards and let out the breath I'd been holding. It's nothing but a pair of inflatable armbands floating on the surface.

My chest is so tight, I could be wearing a corset. Drawing a deep breath through my lips, I fill my lungs then slowly let it out. For a second, the world spins like a merry-go-round. I bend over and fill my lungs once again. Slow, deep breaths, over and over.

Although Joshua shies away from water, I know pools are always a danger to young children. Pools and hot tubs. There's something about the glistening blue water that draws them like a magnet...hot tub! The words trigger a memory of a conversation I had two weeks ago with Mrs. Cooks who'd mentioned she and her husband were having a new Jacuzzi installed on their patio.

Like a sprinter off the starting block, I bolt down the street, vault over the low brick wall in their back yard and dash up the patio stairs. Whipping back a corner of the brown tarp which covers the oversized Jacuzzi, I double over and press a hand to my chest. He's not here.

Pushing the cover back in place, I cast a quick glance into the house. Thankfully, no one is watching me. The muscles in my thighs are burning, and I can hardly catch my breath. Slowly, I straighten up and focus on breathing; in, out, in, out. Gradually, my heart settles back into my chest.

Yet the relief doesn't last long. My child is still missing. Returning to my search, I scan all the neighbor's yards. Like a crime scene technician hunting for clues, I comb every ditch, examine shrubs, check under bushes, and peer over fences, ignoring the spiders, sticky cobwebs, and prickly thorns which would normally make me shy away.

"Joshua!" I call, pausing to listen for the slightest noise. But the only sounds are the steady *tchik-tchik-tchik* of a sprinkler and the distant drone of a lawn mower.

At the end of our cul-de-sac, I turn back toward home. Stumbling up the driveway, my heart is leaden with fear and remorse. What was I thinking? I never should have left Joshua alone in the living-room, not even for a few minutes. In a fit of anger, I kick a grey pebble that has strayed from our pea stone drainage bed. It strikes my Impala with a tiny *thunk*, then drops to the ground. As I stoop to pick it up, I notice a small object near the rear tire. Crouching down for a closer look, I recognize my son's fuzzy, blue slipper.

A sob catches in my throat. Grabbing the handle, I yank the rear door open. Joshua is asleep in his booster seat.

"Thank you, God!" I whisper, slumping against the doorframe.

He looks so sweet, his head drooping to one side, a lock of damp hair dangling over one eye. Mouth wide open, his little chest rises and falls with every breath.

Scooping up the lost slipper, I press it to my cheek. My hands are trembling, my legs are shaking. I need to sit down before I collapse in my driveway. Carefully, I lower myself into the car and rest my head against the seat. Through teary eyes I watch Joshua sleep, my entire being aching with desire to hug him and cradle him against my chest.

"Ma'am?"

I jump, startled to find a police officer looming over me. His name tag reads BOSWELL. "Is everything alright?"

"What – What did you say?" I stammer, noticing the police car parked in my driveway, its blue and red strobe lights heralding its presence to the entire neighborhood.

"Is everything alright?" he repeats, stooping to peer inside the car.

My mind struggles to understand why the police are here. The officer's somber face, the strobing lights, his question, are all too confusing to me.

Setting the slipper onto the seat beside me, I climb out of the car. My legs buckle and the ground rises up to meet me.

The officer swiftly grabs me by the arm and pulls me back up. "You okay, Ma'am?"

"Yes." I sag against the car. "I'm fine."

He frowns. "Maybe you should sit back down."

"No. No. I'm okay."

My gaze swivels to the left as a second officer climbs from the squad car and saunters towards me. His nod is curt.

"Everything okay, Mrs. Raynes?" he asks, hitching up his pants.

My heart skips a beat as I recognize the cropped black hair streaked with grey, the thick eyebrows, and the deep-set eyes, the right one underscored by a jagged scar. Mr. Peterson is a deacon at our church.

Running a hand through my hair, I come away with copper-colored fingers. "Mr. Peterson — I mean Officer Peterson—. "

"We received a call that someone at this address might be in need assistance?"

"Assistance? For what? Who could possibly –?"

Across the street, my elderly neighbor emerges from her home dressed in her floral muumuu. She shuffles across the road, leaning heavily on her cane. Clara! That old coot called the cops on me!

Clara reminds me of a hawk with her beady little eyes and sharp nose. From her living-room window she combs the neighborhood, vigilant and silent, as she watches all the comings and goings, just waiting for something to happen so she can swoop in for the kill.

"Everything okay, Abby?" she asks, her metal cane clunking loudly as she hobbles up the driveway.

There's nothing feeble about Clara. Despite her unsteady gait and frail appearance, she's sharp as a tack. Her husband, Herman, once confided to me that he placed a metal washer in the shaft of her cane so he could hear her coming.

"Forewarned is forearmed," he'd said, winking.

I give Clara a withering look. "Nothing to worry about, Clara."

"Are you the woman who called 911?" Officer Peterson asks, pulling a pen and notepad from his shirt pocket.

"Yes, sir." Clara straightens up as best she can, smooths her short, thinning grey hair, and offers him her best smile. "I heard Abby calling her son, so I came out to see if I could help. Next thing you know, she's trespassing on people's properties, looking in their back yards. It's not the first time her son has wandered away, you know —."

My heart pitches. I can picture the police report; *incompetent mother – son has eloped three times in the past two months – child needs to be placed in foster care.*

Panic wells within me. I feel trapped, like a fly in a spider's web.

"I…I was –."

Two doors down, the Johnson's beagle lets out a deep, resonant howl.

"I was looking for my dog." The fib rolls off my tongue with surprising ease. I'm stunned. It's not like me to bend the truth like this.

Clara snorts. "Your dog?" Her eyes flit back and forth from one officer to the other. "She doesn't own a dog."

Her steely grey eyes lock on mine. "I might be old, but I heard you very clearly. You were calling Joshua's name over and over."

Fear yields to anger. This woman is not going to destroy my family. Stepping closer, I lower my face till it's just inches from hers. "Joshua is right over there, sleeping in the back seat of my car. Go check for yourself."

Clara steps back, but she isn't about to give up. "Perhaps you should keep a closer eye on your son rather than messing with your hair all the time."

Every one of her spiteful words cuts through me like a knife, leaving my confidence as a mother hanging in tatters. I glance at my copper-stained hands. She's right.

Clara turns back to Officer Peterson. "Like I said, it's not the first time she's lost him. Only two months ago —."

"I think we have this under control," he cuts in, placing a hand on her elbow. His voice is calm, yet stern. "The boy is not in any danger, so there's no need to continue this discussion. Would you like some assistance back to your house?"

Clara yanks her arm away and lets out a loud huff. "I can walk home just fine, thank you."

Officer Peterson turns to me. "Glad your son is all right." He pats my arm. "I'll write this up as a misunderstanding between neighbors."

I wonder if he's heard about our situation at church for he appears to grasp what's truly going on.

"Thank you," I whisper. My throat feels like it's closing.

He nods, then climbs into the patrol car. The vehicle emits a short *whoop*, then the strobe lights turn off as the officers pull away.

I turn back toward my own car, struggling against the tears that threaten to betray me. Not out here, in plain view. I need to hold it together until I get Joshua back inside. I let out a deep sigh. That, in itself, could prove more challenging than two police officers and Clara combined.

CHAPTER THREE

Sitting in the back seat of my Chevy, I watch my son sleep. He's a stunning child, with tight blond curls and eyes the color of bluebells. His loveable dimples and a dusting of freckles lend him an air of sweet innocence.

Yet despite this outward illusion of health, Joshua struggles to function in the real world. He battles irrational fears, obsessions, and compulsions. While most children interact with other people, Joshua shies away from them. Unlike typical children who love hugs and cuddles, he shuns human touch. Instead of tickles and peek-a-boos, he favors solitude, fixating on spinning objects such as the wheels on his cars and trucks. Instead of speaking, Joshua remains locked in silence. Autism Spectrum Disorder is the technical label; 'torment' is what I call it.

Scooching closer, I inch my left shoulder under Joshua's sagging head so his cheek rests against me. He stirs, but doesn't wake and, for several blissful moments, I relish the feel of my child's body against mine. How I wish I could pause time right here, in this moment, as I savor this simple, stolen pleasure. But the leather seat sticks to my bare legs and trickles of sweat slither down my back, soaking my pajama top.

I shift, causing Joshua to jerk awake. He sits up, blinks several times, then stares at me, eyes wide. Once again, my brief moment of bliss has been ruthlessly snatched away.

"Hey, Joshua. You fell asleep in Mommy's car," I say, smiling at my little boy.

Joshua glances at the open door, then back at me.

"It sure is hot in here, isn't it? Why don't we go inside and I'll fix you a hotdog and some nice, cold lemonade?"

Joshua throws back his head and lets out a wail, writhing and flailing like a fish caught in a net. His reaction leaves me stunned.

"What's the matter, Joshua?" I say, struggling to make myself heard over his cries.

Joshua's little fingers wrap themselves tightly around his booster seat as he pitches from side to side. Shocked by this intense response, I strive to understand what has triggered the meltdown.

"Want to go to the park?" I ask.

Although it's hot and muggy, a trip to the park is the one bribe that usually entices him to comply.

Joshua rocks harder, fussing and moaning as if he's in pain. Casting a quick glance across the street, I spot Clara's face behind the lace curtains in her living-room window. Most of the neighbors are usually at work at this time of day, so hopefully we merely have an audience of one. Yet I want to find a way to cajole him back into the house of his own free will instead of tucking him under one arm and carting him into the house, kicking and screaming, as I'm frequently forced to do.

Joshua's little hands turn white as he grips the armrests on his new booster seat. We bought it yesterday, after Joshua spotted it at the store; white, puffy clouds against a clear blue sky. His fascination with the weather borders on obsession.

In that moment, I grasp the battle raging in his mind. "Would you like to bring your new booster seat into the house?"

Like the flick of a switch, Joshua stops thrashing. Scooting out of his seat, he grabs the booster chair and clutches it tightly against his chest.

Relief is too slight a word to describe the way I feel as I follow Joshua up the driveway and into the house. Securing both locks behind me, I lodge a chair under the door handle as an extra precaution.

After settling Joshua in the kitchen with a hotdog, a glass of lemonade, and his touch-and-feel book about clouds, I pick up the phone to call Martin.

"Sorry to bother you at work." In the background, I hear snatches of conversation and muffled laughter. He must be at the office. "Joshua disappeared again today."

"What do you mean by disappeared?" Martin asks. I cringe. His voice sounds so loud.

"Shhh!" I hiss. "For Pete's sake, Martin. Do you want everyone in your office to hear?"

"Okay, okay, let me step out for a moment." I hear garbled voices then the thud of a door. "Okay, I'm out in the hall. Now, what did you mean, he disappeared?"

I tell him everything, my words toppling out in a breathless heap; Joshua's escape, my lengthy search, Clara's treachery, even the fib about the dog.

"Martin, I can't do this anymore." I grip the phone like a drowning victim clutches a lifesaver. "We have to figure out some way to prevent Joshua from running off. I'm afraid if he does it again, they will consider us unfit parents and take him away." My sobs recede to whimpers as I slump against the wall and bury my face in my arms.

"Abby, calm down. No one's going to take Joshua away from us. Don't you remember, his case worker told us it's common for children with autism to run off?"

I lapse into silence; even though elopement is part of his autism, it doesn't make it any less of a concern. As his mother, it's my job to protect him and today I failed miserably.

"Tell you what," Martin says. "I'll stop by the hardware store on the way home and grab another bolt lock which I'll install higher up, out of his reach. In the meantime, pull yourself together. Everything will be okay."

I don't know whether to shout or hang up on him. Sometimes his easy-going temperament eases some of the anxiety and worry that are intrinsic to my high-strung personality. Other times, his nonchalant attitude makes me want to scream.

"Abby, I really need to return to the staff meeting. Trust me, everything will be okay."

"Fine," I snap, slamming the phone into its cradle.

This stressful lifestyle is not what I envisioned when I married Martin seven years ago. Back then, I'd idealized the roles of wife and mother but somewhere along the way that idealism tarnished. The harsh reality is that life with autism is a continual struggle. Every day requires relentless stamina and determination just to cope with the demands that dog me from dawn to dusk, and frequently into the night. I can't remember the last time I've slept more than four hours in a row.

Clenching my hand into a tight fist, I punch the wall, fast and hard, gasping as a sharp pain shoots through my hand. Yet it is a welcome distraction from the constant ache in my heart.

A clatter in the kitchen sends me running. Joshua's plate and fork are on the floor and he's standing beside the table, his pull-up and blue pajamas at his feet.

"Hey, Joshua. I see you're ready to get dressed," I say, gathering his plate and fork, then setting them in the sink. "Come on, let's go upstairs and pick out an outfit to wear to the park."

Joshua runs ahead of me, scrambling up the stairs while I collect his discards. Martin's words keep tumbling around in my mind; "Trust me, everything will be okay."

Yet I can't help wondering, what if it doesn't?

CHAPTER FOUR

Convincing Joshua to remove his clothes is easy enough. Given the option, he'd run around all day in his birthday suit. Persuading him to put clothes on is the hard part. Because of his sensory issues, he won't wear anything that isn't cotton or polyester blend. As for tags, zippers, snaps, and buttons, those are simply out of the question.

"What about your Tonka shirt and shorts?" I ask, holding them up for him to see.

Joshua doesn't look at me. He's staring at his hands, his face impassive as he rubs his fingers back and forth in a sifting motion.

"Joshua?"

No response. With a sigh of resignation, I prepare myself for the inevitable struggle which will ensue.

Dressing Joshua is like running with the bulls. I have to be faster, smarter, and two steps ahead of him or I'll regret the aftermath. Sitting on the edge of his bed, I pull him toward me. He resists, then fights to break free as I scissor-lock his legs between my own and wrestle the shirt over his head. Joshua shrieks, then opens his mouth to bite me. I'm a tad quicker, jerking my arm away just in time. Grabbing his left arm, I shove it into a sleeve a second before his head flies back and hits me in the sternum. Oomph!

Gasping with pain, I try to maintain my hold on him. Right now, I feel more like a piñata than a loving mother. Grabbing his right arm, I thrust it into the other sleeve, cringing as his screams grow louder. I loathe this whole process, knowing his sensory issues cause his clothes to feel like an irritant and a constraint, like wearing sandpaper. A memory of the thick mohair sweater my grandmother knit me one Christmas comes to mind. Just the thought makes me itch. Unfortunately, we don't have too many options as far as clothes or no clothes.

Flipping Joshua onto the bed, I pin him down with my leg, dodging his feet as he kicks and flails. With the quick reflexes of a toreador, I shove his right leg into the shorts. Grabbing his left foot as it whips back and forth, I do the same. Clothes on, I finally release my hold. Joshua sags to the floor, then resumes stimming as though getting dressed this way is the norm.

Massaging my sternum, I cross the hall into the bedroom I've shared with my husband for seven years. I love this room with its cream-colored walls and soft-blue accents. Like a harbor, it invites my battered soul to come and find rest.

The large king-size bed dominates most of the room and the thick, white eiderdown and fluffy pillows tempt me into their embrace. But I can't allow myself that luxury while Joshua is up and about. Instead, I focus on getting myself ready.

The oak vanity my mother gifted me waits for me in one corner, its glass top laden with creams, powders, lotions, makeup, and jewelry. Sitting before the mirror, I take stock of the woman gazing back at me. I wince at the worry lines on my broad forehead, the dark circles under my eyes, the uneven streaks of tangerine dye running through my hair. I look like a frightened bird caught in a snare.

Glancing at the framed wedding photo of Martin and me resting on the glass top, I remember how happy and innocent we were back then, ready to take on the world together. Then, three years later, Martin and I discovered we were expecting. We were ecstatic at the news, dreaming and planning for our first child's arrival. Though I struggled through the first couple of months with morning sickness, the rest of the pregnancy was deemed "normal and uneventful." The birth itself was also considered "normal," and, after twenty long hours of labor, I'd delivered a healthy baby boy.

Like a devoted mother, I couldn't snap enough photos our precious little son, shamelessly doting on his perfectly shaped face, his fine blond curls, his soft blue eyes so like my own, and those precious little fingers which wrapped around my finger as though he never wanted to let me go.

But as Joshua changed from a sweet, smiling baby into a fussy toddler, I began to detect subtle changes in his behavior. Seemingly overnight, he ceased making eye contact. It was as though he'd disconnected from the world around him.

When Joshua began crying every time we picked him up or cuddled him, we thought something might be hurting him. His pediatrician assured us there was nothing physically wrong but did recommend we consult a neuropsychologist.

I'll never forget that day. The long, stark hallways at the clinic, the unnerving wait between Joshua's physical exam and his psychological assessment, the whispered discussions between medical personnel as we were handed off from one person to the next, the hard, plastic chairs in the consultation room, the restless pacing as we waited for the neuropsychologist to render a final verdict. When she finally breezed in, she silently extended a hand towards the chairs, inviting us to sit down for the news that would alter our lives forever.

"Your son has Autism Spectrum Disorder," she informed us, her tone as blasé as a waiter reciting the day's specials.

Nothing could prepare us for the brutal shock of hearing the word 'autism' in conjunction with our child. In one fell swoop, all our hopes and dreams were smashed into a thousand tiny fragments. What was once just a word in the dictionary became a living, breathing part of our lives.

Leaning forward, I searched the doctor's face, longing for her to offer some shred of hope, or at least a 'but' to soften the blow. My mind just couldn't accept the finality of such a diagnosis. Instead, the neuropsychologist informed us Joshua would probably remain withdrawn, might never talk, never accept human touch, never be able to care for himself. With every word the knife cut deeper, as though pieces of my heart were being carved out with a dull blade. Unwilling to listen to anymore of her "nevers," I shot from my seat, grabbed my son, and marched out of the room, slamming the door on my way out. We never returned.

That was the day the specter of autism came to haunt my every waking moment. It even troubled my sleep. That day was also the defining moment when I resolved to do everything in my power to release my son from the bondage of autism. I was not going to sit back and let this intruder hold him captive.

As a result, our lives were turned upside down. I found a pediatrician who was willing to work with us, setting up sessions for occupational therapy, speech therapy, dietary counseling, Applied Behavior Analysis, and regular visits with a psychologist who was able to trigger a few minor responses.

Some days we felt a flicker of hope when Joshua responded, or uttered garbled sounds. Those were promising days, much too few and far between. Most days Joshua would experience meltdown after meltdown. Sometimes we could figure out what triggered the meltdown but most of the time we were clueless. When Joshua was in the throes of a meltdown, I had to physically hold him against me, in an arm lock, to prevent him from hurting himself or someone else. If I didn't grab him in time, he'd throw himself down, flailing and kicking, slamming his head against the floor, wall, bed frame or whatever happened to be nearby.

The painful memories draw a deep sigh, producing a sharp pain in my ribs. Joshua's head-butt is going to leave a mark. Reaching for my hairbrush, I gently comb the tangles from my hair, wishing I could do the same with our lives. I braid my hair to cover-up the partial dye-job, then apply a touch of concealer to the bags under my eyes. Unfortunately, there isn't enough makeup to hide the worn-out-mother look I wear most days.

In the closet, I flip through my wardrobe, my choice less dependent on the heat than on its ability to hide the bruises I sport from my son's kicks and punches. I'd be hard pressed to convince anyone I wasn't a battered wife. Opting for a long, sleeveless, cotton print dress with bright yellow sunflowers and a white, lace shawl to cover the marks on my arms, I step out of the closet to find Joshua standing in the doorway.

"Almost ready," I say, smiling at my little boy. No matter what, I love him fiercely, tenderly. Like a mother bear, I will do whatever it takes to protect him.

As soon as I'm dressed, I hold out my hand.

"Let's go," I say, hoping Joshua will reach for it. Yet deep down I'm certain he'll ignore it.

Sure enough, Joshua turns and walks out, his tip-toed gate characteristic of the autism that plagues him.

I trail behind, determined not to cry.

CHAPTER FIVE

Phelps Gove Park is not as large as some of the other parks in Springfield. The massive shade trees and a dozen or so picnic tables scattered across the grassy area seem to appeal to students wanting a peaceful place to study or small groups on lunch breaks. For the most part, this park is quieter than the others.

I've barely pulled into a parking spot when Joshua unbuckles and attempts to open the door. Thankful for child locks, I snag him as he tries to get out.

"Not so fast, Joshua," I say, struggling to secure him into his child-safety harness.

From the depths of my oversized shoulder bag, my cell phone blares *I Will Survive*. Startled, I rustle through my purse, wondering who could be calling. Few people have my cell number other than my husband, parents, and my sister Becky. Digging it out, I glance at the screen to see if it's Mom. She flew to Boston two days ago to be with my sister who's due to deliver her first child any day now.

But the number on my phone belongs to my friend Sarah. We haven't talked in several months.

"Hello?" I say, panting as I juggle my large purse, the diaper bag, the phone, and Joshua's safety-harness.

"Hey, Abby. This is Sarah Whitaker. Did I catch you at a bad time?"

"Not really. I'm at the park with Joshua. What's up?"

"Do you remember Melissa Frazier?"

I comb through my memories of high school and come up with a hazy recollection of a boorish teenager with braces and acne. "Wasn't Melissa the girl who took photos for the yearbook? The one who always had a camera hanging from her neck?"

"Yeah, she was one year ahead of us. She's getting married in three weeks. I know it's short notice, but I'm throwing a shower for her this afternoon, at two. I was hoping you could come."

"I'm not sure, Sarah," I hesitate. "I don't have a sitter and this is sort of last minute."

"Bring Joshua along. It'll be fun. Some of our friends will also be bringing their kids. They can play together while we visit."

Fun? That isn't exactly the term I'd use for Joshua's social encounters. "Challenging" would be more fitting.

Obviously, Sarah senses my reluctance for she puts on a cajoling tone. "Come on, Abby, it'll be like old times. Just us girls hanging out together. Besides, I haven't seen you in so long. Please."

"Okay," I say, though I question my decision. "I may be a bit late, though. I need to stop off somewhere and buy her a gift."

"Fantastic!" she squeals. "I'm so excited! See you at two." The line goes dead.

I stare at the phone in my hand. Have I actually agreed to go to a party with Joshua in tow? I have to be out of my mind!

"Joshua! Slow down!" I say, as he strains on the harness, nearly yanking me off my feet.

It's hard to miss the sideways glances from some of the other parents, the unspoken judgement based upon their perceptions. What they see is a woman yacking on the phone like an irresponsible teenager, her child on a leash. I don't need to read their thoughts to know what they're thinking. It's all there, in the scornful looks they cast my way. What they don't realize is that my child will scream if I hold his hand but, if I release him, he would probably run into traffic. Damned if I do, damned if I don't.

Two young boys rush past and scramble up a tall oak. From the thick, sprawling limbs, squeals of laughter rain down on our heads. Glancing up, I notice several sets of sneakered feet dangling from the branches like fruit on a tree. I look at my son and sigh wistfully. If only.

As we approach the sandbox, I unhook Joshua's harness. I smile at two little boys building a sandcastle, then nod at their mothers supervising from a nearby bench. Without acknowledging me, they drivel on about some new sitcom.

Careful to keep Joshua at a distance from the boys, I guide him to the far end of the sandbox. Sitting on a railroad-tie in the shade of two large sycamores, I watch Joshua scoop up a handful of sand. He stares at his hand as the warm sand trickles through his fingers. He'll do this for minutes on end, enjoying the grainy texture against his skin.

Closing my eyes, I breathe deeply. An unexpected breeze carries the sweet scent of hydrangeas from a bush nearby. It reminds me of Grandma's garden and the wonderful hours my sister and I spent playing dolls in her back yard. Overhead, the flutelike whistle of a thrush fills the air. Slowly, my body and mind unwind. Drawing in several slow and easy breaths, I try to release the negative emotions bottled up inside of me. My shoulders, usually so tense and painful, slowly relax. The headache I've been fighting since this morning stops throbbing against my temple.

36

"Excuse me!" A shrill voice yanks me from my brief respite from reality.

"Joshua! No!" Jumping to my feet, I rush to grab the plastic shovel my son snatched from one of the toddlers.

"Sorry," I mumble, handing it back to the little boy, then crouch down to Joshua's level. "Joshua, you can't take other children's toys. Remember, we've talked about kind hands? That means no pushing or grabbing. You need to play nice or we'll have to leave."

Joshua frowns then glances at the children. He turns and stares at the sandcastle. I snatch him up before he can do any harm.

Joshua lets out an ear-piercing scream and kicks the air.

"In my day, we got a firm swat on the behind," one of the mothers says, as I grab our bags and haul him off.

We've attracted an audience and, even though I keep my gaze averted, I'm aware we're the target of whispers, mostly regarding my son's need for discipline. I know, because I've heard the same disparagements over and over.

"Joshua, stop," I say, trapping his flailing legs under one arm while pinning his chest and arms against me with the other.

We've nearly reached the car and the end of my rope, when Joshua suddenly freezes. Startled, I set him down, worried I might have hurt him. But his gaze is fixed on the far side of the park as he watches a black Labrador Retriever romping amid teens tossing a football.

"Dog," I say. "That's a dog. Like Grandpa's two dogs, Sally and Winchester."

Joshua continues to stare, still as a statue, as he watches the pup run from one boy to the next.

"Look, the dog's having fun with those boys. See how nicely they play? They have nice hands and nice feet, Joshua."

I'm not sure if he's listening, but figure I'll seize the opportunity to bring home a lesson in good manners. I try to nab these teachable moments as often as I can to help Joshua understand proper social behavior, but it's a bit like drilling a hole in a concrete block with a butter knife; it might take a while, but it's the best I can do.

Glancing at my watch, I'm surprised to see it's nearly one o'clock.

"Time to go home and change for Sarah's party," I tell him, pressing the fob to unlock the doors.

I open the rear door but he's reluctant to leave, twisting repeatedly to look at the dog as I press him into the back seat.

"You like that dog?" I ask, buckling his seat belt. "Maybe it'll be here next time we come to the park."

His face relaxes as though the thought brings him happiness. I breathe a sigh of relief as Joshua settles in for the ride home.

CHAPTER SIX

Unlike Sarah, there is nothing unpretentious about her house. The Tudor-style home, with its classic red-brick and stucco construction, its steep, multi-gabled roofs, and four massive brick chimneys, looms proudly at the end of a long drive.

Parking my Impala behind a red Porsche 911, I'm mindful of the Suburban, Lexus, and Mercedes also sitting in her driveway. Obviously, Sarah's circle of friends is vastly different from mine. My fingers grip the keys in the ignition as I sit and listen to the engine tick down. Surely Sarah wouldn't fault me for backing out at the last moment, would she? I'm fairly certain she'd understand if I texted her that Joshua is having one of his terrible days.

A silver BMW pulls in behind me. Glancing in the side mirror, I glimpse a pair of black stiletto heels stepping out of the car, followed by a black sheath dress. I can't see the driver's face because of the enormous gift basket she's holding.

Glancing at my little red gift bag containing a couple of candles, scented soaps, and a $25.00 gift card, I'm tempted to skip the shower and go home. I cast a glance at Joshua sound asleep in the back seat; there's my excuse. I reach to turn the key in the ignition just as Sarah steps out of her house. She greets the woman in the black sheath, then steps aside to usher her guest into the house. She scans the driveway, spots me huddling in my Chevy, and waves.

I wave in return, then mimic someone sleeping, pointing a finger at the back seat. She obviously doesn't understand, for she hurries over to the car and taps on the window. I press the button and it slides down with a *whir*.

"Abby! I'm so glad you came," she gushes. "Come on in."

I place a finger over my lips. "Joshua just fell asleep and I don't want to wake him."

A loud moan emanates from the back seat. I scrunch my face. "At least, he was."

Abby slaps a hand over her mouth, eyes wide as she peers into the back seat. "Oh my goodness! I'm so sorry. I didn't know he was sleeping."

"It's okay. Go back to your guests and we'll be in as soon as he's woken up properly."

"Alright," she says, stepping back from the car. "See you inside."

From the back seat come grunting noises, then the click of a seatbelt being released. After a five-minute power nap, Joshua's up and ready to go.

As soon as I open the rear door, Joshua races toward the fountain gurgling merrily amid a bed of ornamental rockery. My heart skips a beat as he leans in, his feet lifting off the ground as he splashes the water with both hands. Sprinting across the lawn, I grab him around the waist, hoping no one is watching us through the large, leaded glass windows that front the house.

"Come, Joshua. Sarah is waiting for us," I say, setting him down.

Blocking him like a linebacker, I knock on the arched wood door then let myself in before Joshua can break loose and run back to the fountain. As soon as we step into the foyer, I catch a whiff of fresh-brewed coffee and Sarah's fabulous cinnamon cookies. In the background, soft music swells and fades along with the murmur of female voices.

Sarah's house is simply stunning; the walls painted a burnished gold hue, create a warm, welcoming effect that carries through the downstairs and up the wide, sweeping staircase. To my left is an arched doorway, opening into the dining-room, where a twelve-foot table is laden with appetizers, fresh fruit, cheese plates, cold cuts, cookies, a large coffee pot, and several punch bowls. A line of women dressed to the nines snakes around the table, their little offspring alongside them, neatly buttoned up and tucked in.

There is nothing casual about this gathering, as I'd inferred from Sarah's phone call. I stand out like a sore thumb in my simple cotton dress and sandals. I haven't even bothered with my streaky hair, other than braid it. The song *One Of These Things Is Not Like The Others* pops into my head.

Sarah stands in the foyer, talking to one of her guests. She glances up and nods at me. Excusing herself, she hurries over to greet us. Her stunning emerald-green dress matches her eyes to perfection and her long, unruly auburn hair is tamed into a French braid.

"So nice of you to come." She wraps me in a hug, then crouches down to Joshua's level. "You, too, Joshua. I have some toys you can play with. Would you like to see them?"

Joshua grabs hold of my skirt, his gaze fixed on floor.

"It's okay. Mom can come, too," Sarah says.

"You know, it might be best if I just leave Melissa's gift with you," I mutter, grabbing her elbow. "I'm really not dressed for this."

"Oh, phooey! You look fine." As usual, Sarah doesn't seem to notice the disparity between me and the other women. This is one of the traits I love about her; she doesn't care one whit about appearances.

"Come on in and meet everyone," she says, ushering me into the parlor.

The massive room teems with women, none of whom look familiar. Why, oh why did I succumb to Sarah's wheedling? Somehow, I manage to breathe in and out as Sarah leads me through a sea of curious faces, her heels clicking loudly against the hardwood floors.

"Look. There's all sorts of fun toys for you to play with," she says, reaching under an embroidered settee. She pulls out a basket of toys and sets it on one of the oriental rugs strewn around the room. Plucking a miniature pony from the basket, she offers it to Joshua. He looks into the basket instead and pulls out a red car. Flipping it upside down, he spins each wheel, humming as they turn.

Sarah drops the pony back into the basket and pushes herself back to her feet. "He should be happy enough over here. Make yourself at home, Abby. There's plenty of finger foods in the dining-room, so go fill a plate for you and Joshua."

She pats my arm, then strolls off to attend to other guests. Sinking onto the settee, I push aside several yellow and blue flowered cushions and attempt to make myself inconspicuous as I take in the antique chandelier and exposed ceiling beams. Despite its remarkable size, Sarah has managed to make the room cozy. Warm browns, soft creams, and burnished gold hues lend a sense of warmth to the room. Blue velvet drapes, elegant Rosewood furniture, and wood shelves filled with leather-bound volumes complete the mood.

On the far side of the room, a hand-carved, mahogany mantel hangs above an enormous red-brick fireplace. Wedgwood vases line the mantel. In the center, a glass-domed clock chimes two. A pair of upholstered reading chairs gather close to the hearth. I can imagine myself curled up in one of them on a cold winter day, a fire crackling on the grate, a cup of coffee in one hand, a riveting book in the other.

If only.

"Hello, Abby." Melissa Frazier stands before me, a glass of punch in one hand, and a plate of canapés in the other. "I'm so glad you could come."

For a moment, I sit there, mouth gaping. Who is this tall, graceful woman in the Armani sleeveless cocktail dress? Certainly not the homely Melissa I remembered from high school. Somewhere along the way, she's transformed into an attractive and elegant woman.

"Hel...hello," I falter, rising from my seat. "I'm glad Sarah invited me. I had no idea –. "

"We lost touch somewhere along the way," Melissa offers, before popping a cheese cube into her mouth.

I try not to gawk at the enormous princess-cut diamond on her ring finger.

"That's quite a ring," I say.

Holding up her left hand, Melissa tilts it so the diamond catches the sun streaking through the window. "My fiancé Ray picked it out all by himself," she says with a smile.

"He sure did a great job." My laugh sounds flat.

At my feet, Joshua is still engrossed in his game of spin-the-wheels.

"This is my son Joshua. Joshua, can you say 'hi' to Melissa? This party is for her."

Apparently, Melissa isn't as interesting as his car for he ignores her and continues humming and spinning the wheels.

"How old is he?" Melissa asks, her eyes flitting around the room.

I can tell she's already lost interest. Her question is merely polite banter.

"He just turned four," I reply, glancing down at my son who's grunting.

One of the car's wheels has stopped spinning. Joshua frowns as he tries to force it. Recognizing the potential behind that scowl, I crouch down beside him.

"I don't think that car's wheels work very well," I say, offering him a green car. "Why don't you play with this one?"

I spin one of the wheels. "See? This one's much better."

Joshua snatches the green car from my hand and flings it across the room. It hits the hardwood floor with a loud *whack*.

An uncomfortable silence falls over the room. Without looking up, I feel several sets of eyes boring into the back of my head.

"Joshua, we don't throw toys. Please fetch the car you threw across the room."

I realize he won't obey, but I have to salvage my dignity by making some pretense at discipline. If he'd been born with Downs Syndrome or some visible handicap, most people would excuse his behavior, based upon their perceptions. But looks can be deceiving and most of the people we meet out in public aren't so understanding about my son's unruly conduct because his disability is mostly invisible.

I stride across the room, eyes downcast, and pick up the car.

"Sorry," I mumble to the room in general.

I'm not the least bit surprised to find Melissa gone when I return to my seat. *No loss there.* Joshua has resumed spinning the wheels on the red car, humming as he whirls them over and over. I take a deep breath, cross my legs, and swallow my pride.

"Why does he keep doing that thing with the car?" a woman asks. She's claimed one of the comfy wing chairs next to the settee.

I glance at her. I know I've seen her somewhere before. At the moment, I can't remember where or when. For some reason, the name Marsha pops into my head.

"Huh? What thing?" I ask, my mind still scrabbling about for her identity.

"You know, spin the wheels over and over rather than running the cars on the floor?"

Martha! Martha Gibson. The girl with the big mouth who moved here from Maine during our senior year. I never truly liked Martha. Now she's provided me with one more reason.

"He likes the spinning motion," I say, biting down hard on my lip. Why am I constantly having to defend my son's behavior? Why can't someone say, "what a beautiful little boy you have," for once?

"That's kind of weird, isn't it?" Martha's face scrunches up like she's looking at a human aberration.

"It's not *weird!*" The last word comes out louder than I intended. "Unusual, yes. So he likes to watch things spin. What's weird about that?" I can hear my voice growing shrill.

In high school, Martha had never known when to shut up. Why should she be any different now?

"Doesn't it drive you crazy? The humming, the spinning—? "

I jump to my feet, blood pounding in my temples as I struggle with the anger welling up inside. Black spots dance in front of my eyes and the room goes slightly out of focus as I morph into Mom-zilla.

"He has autism, okay?" I blurt out, fighting the urge to clout the woman.

Suddenly, all eyes are on me. Once again, stunned silence has filled the room. I'm not sure if it's pity or judgment I see in their eyes. Or a mix of both. Either way, I can't stay. My son and I don't belong among these women with flawless kids and flawless lives.

Picking up my son, who's still clutching the toy car, I make a beeline for the door. No one says a word. No one tries to stop me. It's probably a good thing. If they do, I might clobber them.

CHAPTER SEVEN

*T*hump. *Thump.*

The noise stirs me from a restless sleep. Prying my eyes open, I glance at the bedside clock. Three a.m.!

Groaning, I toss aside the covers, glaring at my husband who's curled up on his side, mouth ajar, sound asleep. How he can snooze through Joshua's racket every night is simply beyond me. Shoving my feet into my slippers, I yank my satin robe off the end of the bed and stagger from the room, dazed and heavy-eyed.

Thump. Thump.

"Joshua, please stop," I call out, stumbling down the stairs.

I flip on the kitchen light, squinting as my eyes adjust to the glare.

Thump. Thump.

"Joshua," I say softly, kneeling on the cold, hard floor.

No response.

"Joshua, it's still dark outside and you should be in bed."

Absorbed by his current fascination, Joshua pulls repeatedly on the cabinet doors, opening them as far as the rubber bands wrapped around the doorknobs will allow, then grins as they slam closed.

Running a hand through my hair, I make a mental note to ask his occupational therapist for ways to keep him out of the cabinets. So far, he'd broken the childproof locks, so rubber bands are the temporary solution. Not that they're working out that well.

Thump. Thump.

I raise my voice a tad. "Joshua, let's go back to bed."

I touch his arm, ever so slightly. He shudders and pulls away. Every time he does so, it tears at my heart. I understand the words 'sensory disorder,' yet it still blows my mind that my son can't bear his own mother's touch.

I blink back the tears and attempt to come up with a strategy. Perhaps I can entice him back to bed with words in lieu of the warm hugs I'm craving to give him.

"Where's Caleb? Is he still in bed?"

No response. Even the mention of his beloved teddy bear can't stir him from his trance.

"I think I hear Caleb calling your name."

His face is impassive as he reaches for the door handle.

Thump, thump.

"Caleb …," I begin, then stop. Joshua is not listening. I'm wasting my time.

Rising, I grab a glass from the cabinet and fill it with cold water. For some reason, my mouth feels like I've been chewing on sawdust and a dull ache has settled behind my eyes. Tipping the glass to my lips, I take a long, slow drink.

These nightly interruptions are growing harder on me. Tears, which have become so habitual since autism entered our home, fill my eyes. How much longer can I keep living like this, aimlessly running on my gerbil wheel and getting nowhere? I've witnessed so many setbacks and false dawns I'm losing hope and that's a dangerous path to tread.

The silence startles me. I turn to find Joshua has wandered off. Setting my glass beside the sink, I hurry upstairs. He's in bed, Caleb clutched tightly in his arms. Why the boy can cuddle his bear but not his parents makes no sense to me. Then again, nothing truly makes sense with autism.

I breathe out a sigh as I pull the blankets up around his shoulders. No warm hugs. No goodnight kisses. Instead, I whisper, "I love you, sweetie," and blow air kisses.

In the faint glow of his night-light, I stare at the plain walls now stripped of the colorful animals Martin and I had so lovingly painted along the top. The parade of vibrant flamingos, leopards and giraffes that had once marched around the room to climb aboard Noah's ark have been tearfully removed and all four walls painted a drab beige. In one corner, a tall, stuffed giraffe sporting a cheery red ribbon around his neck hunches against the dresser, the only whimsy in an otherwise stark room. Removing the stimulating colors was the first step towards helping Joshua find peace and serenity within his own domain.

These walls aren't the only thing autism has stripped of color. It has robbed me of the bright future I'd envisioned for our family, leaving only bleak prospects for the days ahead. These are dark times, indeed, as I watch Joshua slowly withdraw further and further into his own little world. I fear one day he'll retreat so deeply, he won't be able to find his way back to us. Martin and I need to do something soon, lest we lose him for good.

Pausing in the doorway, I watch Joshua, so sweet in slumber. His hair is getting long and needs a trim, but I can't muster the energy for the struggle that will entail. I'll do it tomorrow while he's napping. As I gaze at my precious little boy, the weight of my sorrow pulls me under. I suck in a deep breath, the strain on my lungs so strong I feel like I'm drowning. Wearily, I stumble back to bed, wondering what today will bring. Probably much the same as every other day. Like a human bowling pin, I rise each morning, dig deep within to dredge up the hope and determination I need to carry me through another day, only to be wacked down over and over again by meltdowns, irrational fears, crazy obsessions, and sheer exhaustion. I wonder how much more I can take before I can't pull myself back up again.

Tossing my robe on the end of the bed, I slide between the sheets. A tear escapes my closed eyelids and slides onto the pillow as I give in to the anguish within me. My heart is breaking. I can't continue like this. The strain is wiping me out.

Like so many other nights before, I cry myself to sleep, my pillow soaked with tears while Martin sleeps on beside me, oblivious to the storm raging within my soul.

CHAPTER EIGHT

The blare of Martin's alarm jars me from sleep.

Beep... Beep... Beep.

It's six a.m. Despite the sun trickling through the blinds, it feels like I've barely fallen back to sleep after my three-a.m. stint with Joshua. Turning my back to the clock, I wait for Martin to shut it off.

Beep... Beep... Beep.

I nudge Martin. He grunts and turns over.

Beep... Beep... Beep.

I briefly entertain the thought of swatting him with my pillow, but that would require too much effort.

"Martin, get up!" I elbow him in the back.

Groaning, he sits up and yawns loudly.

Slipping out of bed, Martin shuffles to the bathroom. Once I hear the shower running, I snuggle deeper under the covers. A few more minutes' sleep wouldn't be unwelcome —.

All too soon, the strong, nutty aroma of freshly brewed coffee lures me from sleep. Slowly, reluctantly, the fog of slumber dissipates along with those happy dreams and random thoughts that usually make no sense at all. The reality of my waking life hits me like a tidal wave. Oh, how I wish I could go back to sleep and wake to a different life, to a better existence. I'm not ready to tackle the demands of this new day.

"Mornin'," Martin says as he sets my *BEST MOM* mug on the bedside table.

I blink as he switches on my reading light. The glare hurts my eyes, awakening the dull ache behind my eyes. I rub my temple several times, then suck in a deep breath. Carefully, I pick up the steaming mug and take a sip. The taste makes my stomach pitch. Shoving aside the covers, I sprint to the bathroom, then drop to my knees and vomit. Kneeling over the toilet bowl, I wonder how much worse life can get.

"You okay?" Martin calls out.

"Just peachy," I groan, grabbing a washcloth off the shelf.

I run it under the cold faucet, then wipe my face. The taste of bile clings to the inside of my mouth. I spit, rinse, then blow my nose. Now it's in my nostrils.

Stumbling back to bed, I crawl under the blankets, wishing I could simply call in sick for the day. But mothers don't enjoy that luxury unless they are in the hospital or dying. Neither one fits my case.

Martin frowns. "How are you going to take care of Joshua today if you're sick?"

I wonder the same thing but can't seem to come up with any answers.

"How about fixing me a cup of tea?" I suggest, mostly to get him out of the room. Given the choice, I prefer to be miserable on my own.

"Gotcha."

Martin grabs my mug, then scoots back downstairs. His voice carries through the vents so, unless he's talking to himself, Joshua must be up already. Does the kid ever sleep?

Eventually, the nausea settles down. I glance at the clock. Shoot! Martin's going to be late for work. Slowly, I sit up and swing my legs over the edge of the bed, hoping my stomach won't lurch back into my throat. I rest there, trying to remember what I ate yesterday. Nothing unusual. Nothing my husband didn't eat too. Hopefully, it's nothing more than a bug. Trusting the worst is over, I slip on my robe and slippers, then shuffle down to the kitchen.

Joshua sits at the table, playing with his bear, Caleb. The Cheerios Martin poured for him rest in the bottom of the bowl. Instead of eating them, Joshua is feeding them to Caleb.

"Good morning, Joshua," I say.

Martin stands by the sink, shoveling a final spoonful of oatmeal into his mouth.

"Oh! Tea!" he exclaims, dropping his bowl into the sink. Grabbing the kettle off the counter, he totes it over to the sink. "Feeling any better?"

"A bit. I'll finish making the tea so you can get out of here."

Martin's shoulders visibly relax as he plugs in the kettle and slips two waffles into the toaster. "I have a sales meeting at seven-thirty this morning, before my regular rounds, so yeah, I need to scoot."

Martin's crazy hours as a pharmaceutical sales rep are another source of stress in our already-faltering marriage. I can never count on him being around for supper or to come home early enough to put Joshua to bed. Most days, I feel like a single mom.

Grabbing my mug off the counter, I pour the coffee into the sink, sighing as I watch the brown liquid swirl around the drain, then disappear down into the black void. Searching the cupboard for some tea bags, I push aside a large red canister of Folgers and half a dozen mugs. They're tucked away in the back, behind the coffee filters. I bought a box of orange pekoe tea for the occasional guest but we haven't entertained any visitors in a while, especially since Joshua started having meltdowns.

"Right. Are you sure you'll be okay?" Martin asks, scurrying back into the kitchen for a quick kiss goodbye. His breath smells like peppermint toothpaste. My stomach roils.

"I'm already feeling much better," I fib. "Don't worry."

Martin glances quickly at the wall calendar. A hemorrhage of red ink bleeds across this month, marking Joshua's numerous doctor and therapy sessions, all attempts to lure Joshua out of his own little world. Attempts that have, so far, done little to improve his chances of ever leading an ordinary life.

"Music therapy and aqua therapy. Looks like a busy day for you two. See you all tonight," he says, waving good-bye.

I watch as the front door closes behind him, then run to the bathroom to throw up.

Some days, life can be brutal. Why should today be any different?

CHAPTER NINE

It's mid-afternoon when Joshua and I arrive at the pool. Between the acute nausea, vomiting twice, coping with three meltdowns, and grappling with an extremely uncooperative child, I'm all done in. Even music therapy, which he normally enjoys, was nothing but a struggle.

As soon as we enter the pool, Joshua cringes and covers his ears. The cacophony of laughter and the children's screams of delight echo throughout the large, open area, assaulting his sensitive hearing. Children in swimsuits, as bright as Starburst candies, race past us on their way to the water slide. Against one wall, parents sit in clusters, chatting while they keep a lackadaisical eye on their kids.

Queasy from the strong vapors of chlorine and the oppressive heat, I pause to collect myself. Joshua huddles beside me, watching the children splashing in the shallow end of the pool. Hands over his ears, his face scrunches up as though he's in pain. A lump forms in my throat. My child is the only who's not enjoying himself.

"Look, Joshua, those children are having fun in the water," I say, attempting to inject a little excitement into my voice.

Joshua remains unresponsive, like a toy without batteries.

"Hey, Joshua!" Annie calls from the roped off lane that's reserved for therapy. "Are you ready to swim?"

Annie, a young woman in her early twenties, has only been teaching aqua therapy for a couple of months. Her bright smile and warm temperament remind me of my childhood poodle, Pooches, who used to welcome everyone with enthusiasm, as though they were the one person he'd been waiting for all day.

Annie casts a glance my way as Joshua stands motionless beside me, locked in silence. While she's comfortable working with individuals with physical disabilities, autism spectrum disorder is a whole different game. Unfortunately, she doesn't realize her charismatic personality scares him.

Lowering myself to the edge of the pool, I dangle my feet in the clear, blue water. It's a tad cooler than I'm accustomed to, yet the slight chill eases the nausea.

"Come on, Joshua," Annie urges, hands outstretched. "Let's have some fun."

Knowing what will happen if she grabs his hand, I slip into the pool and gently tap the surface of the water. "Come, Joshua, Mommy will help you."

Slowly, he tiptoes towards me, his eyes fixed on the floor. He hesitates in front of a cracked tile, sidesteps it, then pauses at the edge of the pool.

"I've got you," I say, arms outstretched.

Joshua has a love-hate response to water. Although he enjoys the weightless feeling it provides, he hates water in his eyes. Aqua therapy is the only time Joshua allows me to hold him.

"Go on, Joshua," Annie coaxes "It's okay."

Joshua glances at her, then stretches his arms out toward me. Wrapping both arms around his little body, I gently lift him into the pool. No words can describe the overwhelming thrill that floods my being as I hold him close.

"That's it!" Annie praises. "Now let's do some leg exercises, shall we?"

I hold him against my body, reluctant to surrender him to his instructor, though I'm aware the whole purpose of aqua therapy is to teach Joshua to relax, develop self-confidence, and learn how to swim.

Annie takes us through the motions, showing Joshua how to kick his feet. But he refuses to let go, clinging to me like a baby koala.

"You'll be okay," Annie tries to convince him. "There's no reason to be scared."

He locks his legs and arms tighter around me, screaming each time she comes near. I must confess, I don't help matters either, caught up in the joy of his embrace.

"Okay, let's work on floating instead," Annie finally concedes.

Turning Joshua so he's facing outward, I press his head onto my shoulder with one hand and support his back with the other.

"Relax, Joshua," I say, as he struggles to right himself. "Use my shoulder like a pillow, and let your legs go."

Slowly, Joshua leans into me, although his arms and legs are stiff as a board.

"Trust me, Joshua," I whisper in his ear. "I won't let you go."

Joshua trusts no one. He's too anxious, too uptight. The world he experiences is too painful and unsafe for him to let down his guard. So when I feel his body slacken, I'm completely taken aback. I shoot a look at Annie; a smile tugs at the corners of her mouth. I return the smile, daring to hope we're witnessing a breakthrough. Or am I merely clutching at straws, fancying hope where there is only longing?

"Look at you, Joshua!" Annie applauds. "You're floating!"

For half a second, I think he's going to break into a smile. But panic overtakes him. His eyes widen and his back arches as he struggles to right himself. Fingers claw the air, searching for a handhold to right himself. In one fell swoop, I scoop him up. He's shaking, his whole body throbbing with fear. Arms and legs wrap themselves so tightly around me, it's hard to take a breath.

"It's okay, Joshua," I whisper, laying my cheek against his head. "Mommy's got you."

Slowly, his muscles loosen up but his grip tightens when Annie suggests he try it again.

"Let's call it a day," Annie says, turning to smile at her next patient.

A middle-aged woman in a fire-engine red swimsuit enters the pool area, pushing a little girl in a wheelchair. She stops at the edge of the pool, scoops her young daughter up in her arms, and walks down the ramp into the water. Lowering her child into the water, she grasps the back of her daughter's life jacket and gently pushes the floating girl towards Annie.

Glancing at my son, I'm reminded I'm not the only one struggling with a disabled child. Other problems, other struggles, yet the same yearning for wholeness and healing.

"You did very well, today," Annie says, turning back to Joshua. "See you next week."

A whole week before I get to hold my son again. Tears well in my eyes, slide down my cheeks, then plummet into the watery depths below. My whole body craves to linger a little bit longer. But the pool will be closing soon and it will take Joshua and me at least twenty minutes to shower and dress.

Now loathe to leave the water, Joshua starts up a slowly increasing wail as we exit the pool and head towards the locker room. Closing the door behind us, I lock it, turn on the shower, and stand under the warm spray with Joshua. I turn off the shower then struggle to peel off Joshua's swimsuit. He's resists me so much, it's like trying to hold on to a slippery fish.

"If you'll quit fighting, we'll stop for ice cream on the way home," I say, tightening my grip.

Joshua continues to howl like a cat that's in heat while straining to break away from my grasp. Dredging up the Sumo wrestler within, I place him in an arm lock, strip off the clammy trunks, then wrestle him into his clothes as he kicks, scratches, pummels, and tries to sink his teeth into my arm.

The first time we attended aqua therapy, one of the pool employees banged on the door, asking if we were okay. Now the staff knows this is typical for him. I quickly shower, then slip into my shorts and tank-top while Joshua stands in the middle of the locker room, emitting a low, strident wail. Shoving our wet swimsuits and towels into my large gym bag, I hoist Joshua onto my hip, collect our belongings, and flee the building.

I've done this same maneuver numerous times, yet it never becomes any easier. And as he gets older, he grows heavier. One of these days, I won't be able to keep the upper hand and one of us will get hurt.

By the time we reach the car, he's completely shut down. Instead of thrashing, Joshua hangs limp in my arms. Unlocking the car doors with my fob, I set him in his booster seat, then buckle him in. He slumps in his seat, silent and impassive.

"I love you, Joshua," I say, leaning in to give him a kiss.

No response. He's retreated into his shell, his safe place where nothing and no one can hurt him.

"Joshua, I love you," I repeat, my eyes misting over. "No matter what, I will always love you."

There's a lump in my throat. Unsure if it's emotion or nausea, I lean against the car, close my eyes, and draw in a deep breath. *One, two, three, four,* I count then slowly release it. In. Hold for four

69

seconds. Out. Finally, the nausea subsides and the tears dry up.

Turning to climb into the driver's seat, I slam my hand hard against the car roof and kick the front tire. Once again, autism carries the day.

CHAPTER TEN

Rather than driving straight home, I swing by the park in the hopes that time in the sandbox will help him snap out of his isolation. Thankfully, there's barely a handful of people at Phelps Grove Park and the sandbox is empty. Joshua has it all to himself.

But as I sit on the hard bench, watching my son silently sift sand between his fingers, I am unable to shut out the squeals of laughter bursting from three middle-grade girls playing on swings behind us. My chest tightens as that familiar pang of jealousy reignites once more. I just wish my son could break free from his fears and the sensory issues which continually drive him back into his shell.

Bowing my head, I close my eyes and cover my ears in an attempt to block out the giggles. I'd weep if I could, but I'm all cried out. My soul is numb. My heart tells me to keep hoping, but my brain presses me to face the ugly truth; one can't live on hope forever.

I jump as something coarse and wet brushes across the back of my hand. My eyes fly open to find a pair of doleful brown eyes gazing up at me.

"Where did you come from?" I ask.

For some reason, the dog standing before me looks vaguely familiar. Could this be the same Labrador Retriever that was running around the park yesterday? I cast a quick glance around the park, but there's no one here other than the girls on the swings.

"Where's your owner?"

The young pup's ribs are noticeable. Her black fur is caked with dried mud and she's not wearing a collar.

"Are you lost, or did someone dump you?"

The dog's panting, making me wonder when she last had a drink of water. As soon as Joshua notices her, a flicker of interest lights up his face. In a flash, he's up and running towards me.

"Be careful, Joshua," I say, holding up a hand in warning. "We don't know anything about this dog."

But Joshua knows no fear when it comes to animals. He strokes the dog, then gives her a pat on the head. With a cautious wag of her tail, she leans into him, triggering a giggle from Joshua. My hand flies to my mouth. This is the first time he's laughed and it's the most beautiful sound I've ever heard. An ember of hope, smoldering for so long deep within my heart, kindles back to life. I'm afraid to move or breathe lest it die out.

Joshua reaches down to hug the dog. She lets out a yip.

"Careful, Joshua," I say, leaning forward. I'm worried the dog might suddenly turn on him. "She might be hurt."

But the pup desperately wants attention. Slowly, she inches towards me, tongue lolling as her soft eyes bore into mine.

"Are you hungry? Thirsty?"

Opening the diaper bag, I root around inside until I find the Ziploc of Cheerios I packed before we left the house. Scooping out a handful, I pour it on the grass near my feet. The dog doesn't wait to be told, but wolfs it down in seconds, then nudges the baggie with her snout.

"Want more?" I ask, pouring out the rest of the cereal.

The food barely hits the ground than it's gone.

"She's pretty hungry, isn't she?" I say, glancing at Joshua who appears to be fascinated by her. "She's probably thirsty, too."

Removing the bottle of Evian I carry in my oversized purse, I pour half of it into the Ziploc, then lean down to the dog's level and hold the bag open for her to lap up the water.

"Hey, hey, slow down!" I say, laughing as she guzzles it down. I'm worried she'll choke.

"You poor dog," I murmur, as the dog, sated at last, sags to the ground.

Joshua plops down beside her, then gently strokes the top of her head like he does with Grandpa's dogs. She appears content just to lay on the grass and soak up the affection.

Over by the swings, the three girls have gathered up their belongings. One of them wanders over, headphones dangling around her neck. She smiles at me, then lowers her eyes to the ground.

"Can I pet your dog?" she asks, half of her face hidden behind a curtain of long, blond hair.

"I was hoping she belonged to you," I say, watching as the girl bends down to stroke the dog. Joshua stares at her for a couple of seconds, then jumps up and runs back to the sandbox.

"Uh-uh. Mom won't let me get a dog. Says they're too much work."

"I'd have to agree with her on that one," I say. "You have to groom them, walk them, feed them, and train them. They're a big responsibility."

The girl shrugs her shoulders. "Not if you enjoy it."

She pats the dog one last time, then pushes herself to her feet.

"Thanks for letting me pet her," she says, then runs off to join her friends.

The dog stands as though she's going to scamper off after the girls. Instead, she trots over to Joshua, her tail wagging back and forth quick as windshield wipers in a downpour. Scooping up a handful of sand, he pours it over the puppy's back. The dog doesn't seem to mind, dropping down beside Joshua, then rolling onto her back, her four legs kicking the air. Gathering another handful of sand, Joshua leans over the dog and pours it on her head. Immediately, the dog jumps up and runs off to the other side of the sandbox, shaking her head, sending sand flying everywhere.

"Don't put sand on the dog's head, Joshua. It hurts her eyes and nose," I say, frowning as he chases her, sand trickling from his fingers. "Besides, the sand needs to stay in the sandbox."

Glancing at my watch, I'm startled it's already six o'clock.

"Oh, hey! It's getting late! Time to go, buddy. Daddy should be home anytime now."

Joshua pays no attention to me, giggling as he chases the pup around and around the sandbox.

"Come on, Joshua. Leave the poor dog alone. Maybe we can come back tomorrow and say hi to her if she's still here."

It's as though I'm speaking to the wind.

"Joshua! Let's go."

No response. I snag his shirt as he runs by, cringing as he lets out a scream.

"Joshua, we have to go home," I say, gripping his hand firmly. I forgot the harness in the car.

Despite Joshua's deafening wail of protest, I catch the *click, click, click* of nails on the path. The dog is following us. My shoulders sag. Although I feel bad for her, I certainly don't want to take her home with us.

"Go home, doggy," I say, waving a hand in the air. "Shoo, shoo."

Instead of running away, the pup catches up with us, tongue lolling out the side of her mouth.

"Go on, shoo," I repeat.

Releasing my hold on Joshua, I clap my hands, hopeful the loud noise will send her running. But this dog doesn't even flinch. She sits and cocks her head, tail thumping loudly on the ground as she gazes up at me with sad puppy eyes.

"Oh, for Pete's sakes!" I grumble. "Shoo means go away, not come hither."

I turn to take Joshua's hand again, but he's run off. Frantic, I cast a look around the empty park, then dash towards the parking lot, praying he hasn't run into traffic. The dog breaks into a gallop, darting past me with a *thrump, thrump, thrump.*

"Joshua! Stop!" I call, spotting him on the other side of the restrooms.

Not only has the dog caught up with Joshua, she's running circles around him, barking and jumping against him. With a burst of speed, I sprint across the lawn and snag my son's arm.

"Don't … ever … run off … again," I pant, feeling like I've just completed the hundred-meter dash.

My shirt is soaked with sweat and my hands are shaking as I push the fob to unlock the car. Opening the door behind the driver's seat, I press Joshua into the car. Instead of obeying, Joshua sags to the ground.

"Come on, Joshua." I can hear the anger in my voice and try to rein in my emotions. "We need to go home now."

I bend to pick him up, but Joshua squirms out of my grasp, jumps up and runs around the front of the car.

"Joshua!" I yell, darting after him.

I manage to grab hold of him on the other side.

"Enough!" I shout. I've lost my cool.

Hoisting him onto my hip, I open the rear door on the passenger side. My stomach clenches as Joshua lets out a shriek. I can only hope his ear-piercing scream doesn't draw any unwelcome attention. I don't need someone to call the cops on me again.

Leaning into the car to set Joshua in his car seat, I'm startled to find the stray dog crouching on the back seat. She must have hopped in the driver's side.

My mouth gapes open. "What are you doing?"

Instantly, Joshua stops screaming and flops into his seat.

"I can't take you home with us," I groan, looking into the dog's gentle eyes. "I have enough troubles right now without taking on a young puppy like you. You're probably not even house trained, are you?"

Glancing around the parking lot, I desperately search for someone, anyone who'll claim this dog. But the lot is empty. There's no one in sight. Even the girls on the swings have gone. I know I can't leave her here, without food or water. In this heat, it won't take long for her to become severely dehydrated.

"Fine," I mutter. "You can ride home with us. But we're going to find your owners. If you have any. If not, we'll have to find someone to adopt you. The last thing I need right now is a puppy."

Slamming both rear doors shut, I slide into the driver's seat, slather my hands with Purex, then start the car. In my rearview mirror, I catch a glimpse of the dog, head nestled on Joshua's lap.

Shifting into reverse, I back out of my parking space. I'm probably making a big mistake. I fear Joshua and Martin will quickly grow attached to the dog and will want to keep her. I don't mind dogs per se, but I am a bit phobic about germs.

I let out a loud sigh. Maybe Dad would be willing to adopt her. Granted, he already has two Australian Shepherds, but he owns a farm so there's plenty of room for another dog. Besides, Dad has a weakness for strays.

I can only hope he'll have a soft spot for this one.

CHAPTER ELEVEN

"**D**addy's home!" I exclaim, as we pull into the driveway.

Martin's Ford Bronco is parked in front of the garage. Maybe he can take the dog to the vet to check for a micro-chip.

I've barely opened the car door than the dog shoots out, like a racehorse out of the starting gate. Her back end wags along with her tail as she heads straight for the grass and relieves herself.

Nose to the ground, she sniffs every inch of the yard. Abruptly, she stops, raises her head as a squirrel darts across the lawn, then lunges after it. With a loud screech, the squirrel zips up our sycamore tree. Perched on the highest branch, it watches the dog circling the base of the tree, scolding her with a loud *Kuk-kuk-kuk-eee, kuk-kuk-kuk-eee.*

"Not even two minutes, and you've already treed a squirrel," I say. "Come here, you silly dog and leave the poor thing alone."

Glancing across the street, I hope to see Clara's face in the window. But there's no sign of her. Her brown station-wagon is not in the driveway either. Figures.

"Come on, puppy," I say, again.

But she's too interested in the chase to listen to me. Not until Joshua darts up the driveway and into the house does the pup abandon the squirrel and bound after him, tail wagging, ears flapping.

"Are my eyes deceiving me or did a dog just go dashing by?" Martin asks, wide-eyed, as I slip past him.

The front door is propped open while he installs the new deadbolt he promised me yesterday.

"She showed up while we were at the park. Poor thing was terribly thirsty and hungry. She looks like she hasn't eaten in a while," I say, setting the booster seat and bags near the door.

He cocks an eyebrow. "I'm surprised. It's not like you to bring home a stray."

"It wasn't my choice," I grumble. "She jumped into the car, then refused to get out. What was I supposed to do?"

"I thought you didn't want a dog?"

"I certainly don't intend to keep her. I'm hoping she has a chip or some identifying marks that might help us locate her owners. Think you could run her to the vet?"

"Not right now. I'm in the middle of this project."

"But the vet will close soon," I say, rubbing my forehead. A pulsing throb starts up in my right temple.

Martin retrieves a screw from his pocket and inserts it into one of the holes on the strike plate. "I'll take her in the morning."

"But –. "

Crash.

I race into the kitchen to find tiny fragments of stoneware scattered across the floor.

"What have you done?" I moan. "That was my favorite fruit bowl."

Tail tucked between her legs, the dog presses up against the doorframe, eyes shifting left and right as though searching for the quickest escape route.

Sucking in a deep breath, I struggle to calm down.

"I don't think I can fix that," Martin says, strolling into the kitchen.

His attempt at humor falls flat. I'm not in the mood for his silly jokes. "Why don't you take her outside before she cuts her paws on the shards?"

"Come on, you little scoundrel," Martin coaxes. "Let's go out back."

With one big bound, the dog launches herself after him.

Thankful to have the kitchen to myself, I sweep the pieces into a pile. I'm about to fetch the dustpan when Martin opens the patio doors to come back inside. Dashing past him, the pup tears through the house and into the kitchen.

"No! No! No!" I yell, as she charges through, narrowly missing the mound of broken stoneware

"Annabelle!" Martin's voice booms through the house. "Come here, you little varmint!"

I raise my eyebrows when he appears in the doorway. "Annabelle?"

"Well, she doesn't have a collar or tags, so I'm testing various names to see if she responds to any of them. Thought I'd start at the beginning of the alphabet."

"Oh no! No, no, no!" My voice grows shrill as the dog jumps up against the marble counters and sniffs at the canisters.

"Down!" I say, pushing her paws off the countertop. "Martin, why did you let her back inside?"

"She's thirsty, honey." Martin pulls a metal mixing bowl out of the cabinet and fills it with cold

84

water. "She needs water if she's going to be outside, especially in this heat."

"Not my mixing bowl!" I yell. "What are you thinking?"

"What do you want me to use, then?" Martin says, throwing his hands in the air.

"How about an empty ice-cream container? There's several in the pantry."

Grumbling something about obsessive and germs, he grabs a plastic ice-cream bucket and fills it with water.

Dustpan in hand, I turn to sweep up the pile of broken pottery only to discover the dog has her head buried in the garbage can. Several wrappers and an empty can of tuna lay at her feet.

"Get your nose out of the trash!" I holler.

Startled, the dog raises her head then backs away, cowering behind Martin as she licks her lips.

"I guess we'll have to feed her something," I admit. "For now we can give her last night's chicken and rice, but you're going to have to make a run to the store for some regular dog food." Martin scowls and pinches his lips together as he retrieves the leftovers from the fridge and dumps them in a second plastic bucket. I must be trying his patience

"Uh-uh," I say, as he bends to set the buckets on the floor. "Outside."

With a scowl and a shake of his head, Martin calls the dog. "Come on, Bridget. Tonight's dinner is al fresco."

"Bridget is not a dog name," I call out, as Martin heads out back, both buckets held high as the dog leaps against him, trying to get to the food.

I crank the window to let in some fresh air, as I fill my cleaning bucket with water and floor-cleaner. The lemon scent is a bit overwhelming with my stomach still unsettled. Outside, the steady *tap, tap, tap* of a pileated woodpecker draws my attention. I frequently spot him in my neighbor's sycamore tree, searching for tiny insects to eat. Its flaming red crest bobs up and down as it bores fresh holes in the tree limbs.

In some ways, he reminds me of myself and my own incessant quest for answers. I keep pecking away at the same issues and struggles, unwilling to give up, hoping to uncover some new therapy or treatment which might help my son. Yet most of the time my efforts yield nothing but false hopes.

A swell of sadness rises in my chest and settles there like weight. Some days, I wonder how much longer I can continue in this futile modus operandi. Something has to change, and soon.

CHAPTER TWELVE

Once the kitchen is finally scrubbed clean, I take a sponge from under the sink, fill a pail with warm water, then add a squirt of Dawn dish soap. If that dog stays here tonight, she'll need a bath.

As I slide open the patio door and step outside, the pup comes bounding over, jumping against me, eager to check the contents of my pail.

"Get down!" I say in a no-nonsense tone of voice. "I don't have any food. This is just bath water."

She sniffs the bucket, sniffs my hands, then jumps down. Her rear-end shakes with excitement as she circles me.

"Sit!" I say, sharply.

She drops to the ground, ears lowered, tail tucked between her legs.

"It's okay," I say, softening my tone. I feel bad I frightened her.

Hesitant, she sits up and looks at me, as though trying to gauge my mood.

"It's okay, sweetie." I set down the bucket of soapy water.

Curious, the dog sticks her head in the bucket, then yanks it out, her muzzle white with suds.

"No! This is not for drinking," I laugh, wiping the shiny bubbles off her muzzle. "This is for bathing."

I look up to find Martin watching me with the quirky, lopsided grin that reminds me so much of Nathan Fillion. In certain ways, he reminds me of the movie star from *Castle*, with his round face, short caramel-colored hair, and piercing blue eyes that light up when he smiles.

"Care for some help?"

"No," I say with a touch of humor in my voice. "I thought you might enjoy watching me struggle with this big, dirty lump of fur."

"Come here, Clarence," he says, patting his leg.

The pup sidles up to him and leans into him. She obviously likes my husband. I don't think she's too sure what to think of me yet.

"Clarence is a masculine name," I say, dipping the sponge in the soapy water. "In case you hadn't noticed, this dog is a girl."

She doesn't protest when I squeeze the sponge, releasing warm water across her back. Dirty water trickles from her coat onto the brick patio.

"This is exactly why you're getting a bath," I say, lathering her legs and torso.

A mixture of water, mud, sand, and dried grass pools at her feet. Her fur is no longer sooty-black. Instead, it reminds me of the soft, black velvet lining my jewelry box.

"Obviously, no one's taken care of you in quite a while," I say, patting her head.

Joshua suddenly lets out a strident wail.

"It's okay, Joshua. Mommy isn't hurting the dog," Martin says, struggling to make eye contact with his son. "See? She likes her bath. Want to help?"

Joshua's howls weaken to a snivel. He shuffles his feet, then edges closer to me. I hand him the sponge and point to the pail.

"Dunk it in the water first," I tell him.

He wipes his nose with the back of his hand, then dunks the sponge in the pail. Water dribbles through his fingers as he lifts the sponge over the dog's shoulders and squeezes it

"Good job, Joshua!" I say, clapping.

A timid smile plays at the corner of his mouth. I cast a quick glance at Martin. He's holding his smart phone in one hand, recording this extraordinary development. Given his inclination to dissociate from the world around him, it's startling to see Joshua interact willing with us like the average child. This is one of those heart-stopping moments that leaves me feeling giddy with hope.

Once is enough for Joshua, who drops the sponge in the pail, then wanders off to spin the wheels on his toy truck. I tuck this precious memory in my mind. Thankfully, Martin has recorded it, a tangible reminder that my little boy is still reachable.

The dog appears to be losing interest, for she sags to the ground and flops on her side. I quickly run the sponge over her a couple more times, until the water runs clear.

"I haven't seen that smile in a while," Martin says, a playful look in his eyes. "You seem to be enjoying yourself."

"I guess I am." I smile back at him. "Silly, isn't it?"

"No, it's not silly," he says, laying a hand on my shoulder. "Think of it as a blessing. Anything that brings you joy is a blessing."

He leans in to kiss me. As I close my eyes and purse my lips, the dog jumps and shakes herself dry.

"Oy!" I squeal, jumping back. "Shake yourself somewhere else!"

Our eyes meet and we erupt into giggles.

"You look like a drowned rat," I say, chuckling at his soggy hair and damp shirt.

"Speak for yourself," Martin says, using the hem of his shirt to wipe his hair dry.

Unfazed by our reaction, the pup lopes across the lawn, then flops on the grass and rolls around on her back, all four legs in the air.

"Hey, I just washed you!" I say, elbowing Martin who's laughing so hard, big, fat tears roll down his cheeks.

"I'm so glad you brought her home," Martin says, wiping his eyes. "I haven't laughed this hard in a long time."

I nudge him. "Don't get too used to it. She probably has a family and a home."

A shadow crosses his face. He turns away and my heart plummets. Why did I have to bring that up and ruin the mood? Snatching up the pail, I dump the dirty water on the lawn, then walk back into the house, wishing I could take back my insensitive words.

CHAPTER THIRTEEN

There was a time I enjoyed working in the kitchen, creating balanced meals, and trying new recipes. But lately, I spend so much time driving my son to his various appointments and therapies, I just don't have the time or the energy to fix anything that requires more than five basic ingredients. Besides, I can count on one hand the foods Joshua will eat which makes it a challenge to come up with tasty and nutritious meals.

"Time for dinner!" I call, sliding the patio doors open.

Martin and Joshua are running around the yard, the puppy scampering after them, barking her pleasure. She's trying to steal the tennis ball out of Martin's hand. I laugh gently, thinking how wonderful it appears, the picture of an everyday, ordinary family playing together in the yard. Yet I know how fickle moments like these can be. *If only this could be my reality instead of a rarity,* I think, letting out a big sigh.

Martin tosses the ball and, with one swift leap, the dog snatches it in her mouth, then muscles her way past me into the house.

"Stop!" I cry, rushing after the dog. Without a collar, it's hard to grab her. "Come back here!"

Capturing this bundle of fur is a challenge. She's cunning and she's fast. Tail whipping back and forth like a garden hose, she darts through the living room, then takes a sharp turn into the kitchen. The slick tiles catch her by surprise and she skids across the floor, crashing head-first into the cupboards. Stunned, she lays there for a brief moment, then scrambles to her feet, her soft paws flailing as she scrabbles for purchase.

Lunging after her, I manage to clutch a handful of fur. "Gotcha!"

She obviously thinks this is a game for she bolts towards the stairs, towing me along behind. I lose my grasp and watch in dismay as she barges up the stairs.

"Martin!" I yell.

But he's already on it, taking the stairs two at a time in hot pursuit. I hear pounding feet, a crash, then silence.

"Are you okay?" I call up the stairs.

No response.

"Martin?"

At last, he appears at the top of the landing, carrying the furry runaway in his arms. "I knew those tackling drills in high school would come in handy someday."

The dog licks Martin on the ear and barks her pleasure as he totes her downstairs, then sets her down in the back yard.

"Stay!" he says, holding up his palm.

Backing into the house, he quickly slides the glass doors shut. The dog nuzzles the bottom of the door, then gives us a pitiful look, nose pressed to the glass.

"Well, that was fun, wasn't it?" Martin says, strolling into the kitchen to wash his hands.

I roll my eyes as I set a dish of macaroni and cheese on the table. The creamy, cheesy goodness in the middle and golden crispiness on the top makes my mouth water. I add two small bowls of salad for my husband and me, then call Martin and Joshua to the table.

Dropping into his chair, Martin raises his glass to his lips and takes a sip. The screech of nails on glass sends water spewing from his mouth.

"For goodness sake," Martin says, leaping to his feet.

"What are you doing to my doors?" I hear him bellow from the living room, as the patio doors slide open. Seconds later, he returns, the dog bounding along beside him.

"Did you really have to let her back in?" I say, frowning.

Martin plops into his chair. "I don't have much choice, honey. With her sharp nails, it won't take long for her to scratch up the glass doors."

Without a word, I dish out three servings of macaroni and cheese. The throb in my temple is starting to flare up again. As I slide into my seat, I glower at the dog who's huddled against Martin, her head resting in his lap. She glances at up me, her brown eyes bright with contentment.

"Don't get used to it," I grumble, stabbing my fork into my salad. "This doesn't end here."

As soon as supper is over, Martin scoots off to the pet store while I put dinner away and load the dishwasher. I've barely finished wiping down the table and counters when he returns, loaded down with two large paper sacks and a twenty-pound bag of dry dog food.

"What's all this?" I ask.

One by one, Martin pulls items from the bags.

"Two stainless-steel dog bowls, one for food and one for water, a pink collar, a regular leash, a retractable leash, a harness, some dog biscuits, treats to reward good behavior, rawhide bones to appease her urge to chew on things, dog shampoo, nail clippers, a padded dog bed, and a toy duck that squeaks. Listen."

He squeezes the duck which emits a garbled squawk that sounds more like a chicken than any duck I've ever heard.

I pinch the bridge of my nose. "I thought we agreed she would stay here just until we find her owners or we find a family willing to adopt her."

"I know, I know," Martin says, looking a bit sullen. "But I figured she could use a little pampering after what she's been through. Besides, if she –."

A trickling sound stops him mid-sentence. We both wheel around to find our little orphan peeing on the kitchen floor.

"No, no, no!" Martin cries. "Not in the house!"

With uncharacteristic speed, Martin scoops her up and rushes to the back door, holding her at arms' length. "Outside! You pee outside!"

I close my eyes and rub my temple. What have I gotten myself into?

"I think I startled her enough to stop her mid-flow," Martin says, strolling back into the kitchen. "Hopefully, she'll finish her business outside."

With a swift flick of the wrist, Martin yanks a paper towel off the roll then wipes up the small puddle in front of the trash can.

"There we go," he says, smiling. "All taken care of."

I shake my head in disbelief, instantly regretting it as a sharp, stabbing pain shoots through my skull.

"Think I'll go put this collar on her while she's outside. Then we'll have something to hold on to, should she decide to tear through the house again," Martin says, strolling out of the kitchen, the bright pink collar clutched in his hand.

Gathering the mop and bucket, I scrub the entire floor several times, just to be sure. Call it obsessive, but I won't be able to rest until I'm sure my kitchen is sanitized.

CHAPTER FOURTEEN

"Where's Joshua?" I ask Martin.

My husband is comfortably settled in his recliner, watching a baseball game with his feet up, a bag of chocolate chip cookies in his lap. The Springfield Cardinals are playing the Dodgers.

I've run Joshua's bath and set out his pajamas. Now I just need to convince him it's time to get ready for bed. His matchbox cars are lined up on the living room floor. Every evening, after supper, he sets them up in the same, identical pattern. Whenever Martin or I buy him a new one, he adds it to the end of the queue. He currently owns fifty-two cars. It blows my mind that he remembers the sequence.

"Martin?"

Martin jerks at the sound of my voice and looks up. "What did you say?"

"Do you know where Joshua is?"

Martin points towards the kitchen. "Last I saw, he and the dog were heading that way."

I shudder at the way my husband goes about his parenting responsibilities. His insouciance is amazing, considering the number of times Joshua has run off or gotten into some type of mischief. Maybe that's why he's still sane while I'm falling apart.

At first glance, the kitchen appears to be empty. But a faint nibbling noise catches my ear. Crouching to look under the table, I spot the pup laying on the floor beside Joshua. Both of them are munching on dog biscuits, the open box beside them.

"Martin!" I yelp, staring wide-eyed at the scene before me.

Why is my picky little eater chewing on a dog biscuit when he won't even eat most foods children love? This child is one big bundle of contradictions.

"What?" Martin shouts from the living-room.

"Get in here!" I yell, my patience wearing thin.

Martin lumbers in, the remote in one hand, a chocolate-chip cookie in the other. "What?"

"Look under the table."

Slowly, Martin bends over, then lets out a bark of laughter. "Oh, this is good. This is good. Make sure they stay there while I grab my phone. I've got to get a video of this."

I can't believe it. My husband thinks this is funny! Crawling under the table, I grab the box of biscuits then fumble my way back out. I'm worried

Joshua could ingest something harmful. Flipping over the box, I check the list of ingredients; malted barley flour, egg, salt, liver powder, oats…. The list goes on and on.

"Can you scoot left just a tad?" Martin says, crouching beside me. He points his smart-phone at Joshua and the dog, his face bright with humor.

With a grunt, I heave myself off the floor and hurry to the phone. A bright red poison helpline sticker on the landline tells me to dial 1-800-222-1222. My hands are shaking so badly, I find it tricky to punch in the numbers. A pleasant, soothing, female voice comes on the line.

"Poison control center, how may I help you?"

"My son just ate a dog biscuit," I wail, tears filling my eyes. My legs wobble. Back against the wall, I slide to the floor.

"What brand of dog biscuits?" the woman inquires.

I rattle off the brand and type of biscuit.

"He should be just fine, ma'am. Does your son have any food allergies?"

"No, no he doesn't." My heart rate begins to slow as her words sink in.

"If you have any concerns or questions about what he's ingested, you might take him to the nearest

Emergency Room or call your physician. But dog biscuits are generally not harmful to humans."

I glance up, surprised to find Martin leaning against the doorframe. His brow is creased with worry. I drop my eyes, reluctant to meet his gaze.

"Thank you." I choke out the words, then hang up.

I close my eyes and take in a deep breath, leaning into the cold, hard wall behind me.

"Did you just call poison control?" Martin asks, lowering himself to the floor so he's sitting across from me.

"Yes," I say, curtly, hoping to discourage further questions.

"Oh, honey," he says, scooting closer. His strong arms wrap me gently in a hug. The tears I've been holding at bay for so long break free and course down my cheeks. This is exactly why I didn't want to tell him.

"Dog biscuits won't hurt our son."

"How do you know?" I snap, pulling away from his embrace.

I don't want him to comfort me. It's easier to keep him at arm's length so my emotions remain carefully boxed up. "Just because it's safe for dogs doesn't mean it's safe for human consumption."

Pushing myself to my feet, I pick up the box of treats and head into the kitchen. Placing the dog bones on top of a cabinet, I squat down to peer under the table. Joshua is curled up on the floor, arms wrapped around his furry buddy. All traces of the biscuits are gone.

"Come on, Joshua. It's time for your bath."

No response.

"Joshua, it's bath time," I repeat.

This day has sucked a great deal out of me, physically and emotionally. I'm half tempted to skip the whole bath-time routine for once. But the tub is full and the thought of Joshua going to bed with today's dirt still on his body is simply unacceptable.

"Martin, would you please get Joshua out from under the table? I'm going upstairs to add a bit of hot water. The bath's probably cold by now."

My feet feel like lead weights as I mount the stairs. How I wish I could simply go to bed. My head is pounding and my stomach is still queasy. Dipping a hand into the tub, I test the water. It's still fairly warm. Downstairs, a series of loud screams erupt. Heart racing, I pound down the stairs to find my son running in circles, howling like a cyclone.

"What happened?" I yell, reaching out to nab Joshua as he whips by.

Martin points towards the cars, strewn across the floor. "The dog accidentally knocked them over and he flipped out."

I manage to snag Joshua by the arm and pull him against me. Locking my son in a strong hug, I wait as he thrashes and flails his arms.

"When you stop struggling, I will let you go," I say, fully aware physical touch exacerbates his stress. Unfortunately, it's the only way to prevent him from harming himself. Gradually, his cries dwindle to a whimper. I release him and he sinks to the floor.

My head feels like it's about to burst. "Come on, Joshua, let's get this bath over with."

Like an automaton, Joshua follows me upstairs. I add hot water to his bath while Joshua shucks off his clothes. Silent, he climbs into the tub, then lowers himself into the water.

"Joshua, it's okay," I say, squeezing liquid soap onto a washcloth. "Relax."

He stares straight ahead, his body rigid.

"Remember how much the dog enjoyed her bath today? You were such a great helper."

Joshua looks intently at the plain white tiles on the wall. He flinches when I wipe his back with the washcloth. It pains me to see how sensitive he is.

"Now your hair," I say, bracing for the inevitable struggle.

Joshua curls into a little ball and shies away from me.

"Come on, Joshua. We do this every night."

Water sprays across the room as Joshua kicks his feet and flails his arms.

"Stop it, Joshua!" I shout, slumping against the tub.

"Who's taking the bath, you or him?" Martin grins from the doorway. I hadn't heard him come up.

"Some days I wonder why I even bother." I snatch up the washcloth and, with one swift movement, run it through his hair. Joshua kicks hard and fast, sending a huge spray of water in my face.

"Joshua!" I sputter, jumping to my feet. I'm drenched and ready to scream.

Snatching a towel off the linens shelf, I wipe my face and pat down my hair.

"Oh, by the way, your mom just called," Martin says, turning to leave. "I told her you'd call back as soon as you get Joshua to bed."

I lower the towel and stare at him, slack-jawed. "You couldn't take over so I could talk to my mother? For Pete's sake, Martin! Becky is due any day now. You'd think –."

Joshua stands, and lifts one leg over the edge of the tub. I grab him around the waist and lift him out, worried he might slip and bang his head.

"Never mind." Taking Joshua's towel off the rack, I quickly wrap it around him. "That's the whole problem. You don't stop to think."

I shoulder past him, steering Joshua towards his bedroom. After coaxing him into his pajamas, I tuck him into bed.

"Want to read *Goodnight Moon*?" I ask, reaching for his favorite bedtime story.

Joshua doesn't respond. Instead, he gathers Caleb into his arms and cuddles him to his chest. I settle beside him, my head close to his as we lean against the headboard. What I really yearn to do is to snuggle with him, to hold him close and drink in his unique smell mingled with the bubble gum-scented bath soap still lingering on his skin and damp hair.

"In the great green room there was a telephone –." I begin.

A blur of black fur streaks into the room and pounces on the bed with a heavy *whomp*.

"Oof!" I yelp. "You're not allowed up here. Get down."

The dog flops down between us, gazing at me with doleful eyes.

"Come on, get down," I repeat, my tone stronger, firmer.

She scooches closer, then lays her head in my lap.

"No. None of that," I groan, pushing her off me. "You don't listen very well, do you?"

She cocks her head and, despite my frustration, I can't help but laugh at her antics. "Yes, I know you like being with us. But you belong outside, not on the bed."

"Martin!" I yell loudly, hoping my voice will carry downstairs. "Martin!"

Joshua leans over and wraps both arms around the dog's neck, burying his face in her fur. Watching my son snuggle with her tears at my heart. While I realize she makes him happy, I simply can't bring myself to let her sleep in his bed. It's not just the fur all over the sheets and blankets, it's also the dirt, the possibility of fleas or ticks, never mind the communicable diseases dogs carry.

Finally Martin saunters in, TV remote still clutched in his right hand. "You called?"

"Could you please get this dog out of here?"

"Come on, puppy," he says, patting his thigh.

Immediately, the dog jumps down and follows him out of the room.

"Unbelievable!" I mutter, staring after them.

"Now where were we?" I say, holding the book so Joshua can see the pictures. "In the great green room –."

As soon as we are done reading, Joshua curls up on his side, Caleb nestled against his chest.

"Goodnight, Joshua," I whisper, tucking the blankets around his shoulders.

I turn off his bedside lamp and, in the dim glow of his nightlight, watch my little boy as he nestles down under his blankets. I wonder what the future holds for him. Will he ever speak or play with other children? Will he eventually accept our touch or be able to socialize? I have so many questions, but far too few answers.

With a heavy heart, I stagger down the hall to the phone. Much as I want to fall into bed and go to sleep, I ache to know if Becky's in labor.

"Mom?" I say, as soon as she picks up. "It's me."

"Hi, honey." Mom's voice sounds agitated. "I'm so glad you called back."

A rush of worry hits me. "What's the matter?"

"Nothing, actually. Becky's baby seems rather content to stay where she is."

"Then why do you sound so stressed?" I ask.

"I'm worried about your father. I just talked to him and he sounded distracted. I don't like to leave him alone for too long. Are you still planning to visit him on Sunday?"

"Absolutely." I'm unable to stifle the yawn.

"You sound tired."

"Yeah." It's all I can say without losing it. The last thing Mom needs right now is a blubbering, hysterical daughter.

"Get some sleep, honey. I'll call you again tomorrow."

"Thanks for calling, Mom. Tell Becky I'm rooting for her."

"I'll let her know. Goodnight, sweetheart. I love you."

"Love you, too."

As soon as I hang up I unravel like a skein of yarn caught on a nail. Burying my face in my hands, I cry out the fatigue, stress, and frustration that has been building up inside me throughout the day.

Tears spent; I drag myself off to bed. Out of habit, I look in on Joshua. At some point, the dog scooted back into his room. Joshua is sound asleep, his right arm and right leg draped over the dog huddled alongside him, like a hot dog in a bun.

Despite my concerns, I can't dredge up the energy to struggle with the dog again. I'm beyond exhausted and my head is about to split in half. I have to admit, they do look cute snuggled up together like that.

Acknowledging a temporary setback, I turn and shuffle off to bed, eager to put this day behind me.

CHAPTER FIFTEEN

The doorbell rings, causing me to drop the fitted sheet I just stripped off Joshua's bed. I can't remember the last time someone used it. Using the side of my foot, I nudge the sheet onto the growing pile of linens, then hurry downstairs.

Peering through the peephole, I'm startled to see Sarah on my doorstep. My stomach tightens and I let out a muffled moan. I am not ready to talk to her yet. I'm still embarrassed about the way I acted at the party.

Drawing in a deep breath, I steel myself and open the door.

"Come on in," I say, unable to meet her gaze.

Sarah steps into the hall, placing her purse on the floor next to the console table. There's a beat of silence as we stand there, staring at the floor.

"I –," Sarah begins.

"What –," I start.

We both let out an awkward laugh.

Sarah reaches out, touches my arm. "I came over to apologize."

My head snaps up. I look into her eyes which are brimming with tears.

"I was wrong to push you and Joshua into a difficult situation. I should have known better."

I reel back, as though she's slapped me. Criticism I can deal with. I've grown accustomed to it. Kindness is a different matter.

"I'm sorry I ruined your party," I offer.

"You didn't ruin it," Sarah says. "After you left, I explained about Joshua's autism. Everyone seemed to understand."

I have a tough time believing that. In my mind, I can hear the whispers. "Oh my, how sad. I can't imagine –."

I turn away. "Come on in. Joshua will be pleased to see you."

Stepping over the wood blocks Joshua is setting in a straight line; I flop down on the sofa.

"Hey, Joshua." Sarah squats down.

Joshua continues with his task without looking up.

Sarah stands, then comes to sit beside me. "Like I said, I shouldn't have insisted you come to the party. You weren't ready for it, and neither was Joshua."

For several moments, we sit in silence, the air between us growing heavy and uncomfortable. In my lap is a tissue I've balled into a tight wad.

"Can I speak candidly?" Sarah plucks a speck of fuzz from her black slacks then turns to face me.

Every part of me wants to cry, "No!." She's treading a minefield; one wrong word and I might explode.

"Your son's autism has really changed you, Abby. You're so worried what people think of you and Joshua that you can't relax and have a good time. Unfortunately, you're shutting everyone out in the process."

I swallow hard. Her words hit like a punch to the gut.

"Martha felt terrible. She didn't mean to upset you. I know at times she can be blunt, but maybe you could have clarified Joshua's behavior, instead of lashing out at her."

"Perhaps she should have kept her big mouth shut," I snap. I'm surprised by the intensity of anger and resentment churning inside me. "You come to my house to apologize, then tell me how to parent my kid. That's a bit ironic, coming from someone who doesn't have a child of her own."

She winces. "I didn't come here to fight –."

In a flash of rage, I hurl myself off the sofa and stagger across the room. Yanking open the patio door, I stumble into to the back yard, then slam the door shut behind me. How dare she come into my house and tell me how to live my life?

Part of me is tempted to storm back into the house and order her out. She's crossed a line. Why should I have to put up with her criticism and unsolicited advice? What does she know about raising kids or coping with autism? After all, she doesn't even have any kids. She spends her days however she wants, travels overseas with her husband when she so chooses, and lives a carefree existence. I find it a bit ironic for her to tell me to just relax and have a good time when she probably has no idea what stress even looks like. I have every reason to be angry with her.

Then why do I feel so guilty?

Pacing around our tiny backyard, her words keep pecking at my mind. *You are shutting everyone out in the process.* True, I'm on edge, but aren't I entitled to an occasional outburst?

You are shutting everyone out.... Your son's autism has really changed you.... Truth is, I barely remember the woman I was. My son's diagnosis effectively split me into two distinct persons; the woman I was before autism, and the one I've become.

Sadly, I'm unwittingly falling into the same erroneous behavior pattern I've struggled so hard against with Joshua; in an effort at self-protection, I'm pulling away from anyone and anything that threatens my little world. Joshua's autism and my overly-protective behavior have become walls we've erected in order to shield ourselves from the harshness of a world which doesn't understand us.

I wonder where my old friends have gone. Somehow, I've failed to keep track of them and let them steal away to places unknown. They've moved on, while I huddle behind my walls, keeping everyone at a safe distance. Even my best friend, Sarah.

With a scorching sense of shame, I glance inside. Sarah sits on the floor across from Joshua. She picks up a red block, stacks it on top of a green one, then points to a blue block. Joshua picks it up, the tip of his tongue touching his lower lip as he carefully places the blue block on top of the red one. The tower crumbles.

Sarah laughs and claps her hands. Joshua stares at her in surprise. I watch, holding my breath, waiting for the inevitable meltdown. Now she'll see why I'm always so uptight. Instead, Joshua grins at Sarah, picks up a yellow block, and starts rebuilding the tower.

My hand flies to my mouth. I'm completely taken aback. Why didn't Joshua have a meltdown?

Have I grown to expect it? Am I enabling him? Maybe I'm going about it all wrong. My sense of inadequacy as a mother surfaces and all the self-doubts I'm constantly fighting off return with a vengeance.

I swallow the lump clogging my throat as I take in the scene unfolding inside. From the looks of it, Sarah is building a castle. Silently, Joshua watches her every move. Every so often, she pauses, hands him a block, then shows him where to place it. Slowly, carefully, he sets it in the proper spot, then sits back with a look of satisfaction.

How can I stay annoyed with her when she's so good with Joshua? My angry words have left a bitter taste in my mouth. I need to set things right and apologize to her. After all, she's my best friend. Possibly the only friend I have left.

CHAPTER SIXTEEN

"Why don't you get out the house for a bit?" Sarah takes a sip of orange-pekoe tea, then sets her cup in the saucer, leaving a streak of pink lipstick along the rim.

When I eventually came back into the house after stomping out my anger, I'd avoided the topic of Sarah's party. Instead, I'd offered her a drink as a truce.

"Go where?" I ask, raising my teacup to my lips. I take a sip and wrinkle my nose at the sharp aroma of orange and zesty spices.

"Out. Anywhere. To the shops, the mall. Just to get away from the house."

"I don't have anyone to watch Joshua," I argue. "Martin's at the vet with a stray dog we found yesterday, checking to see if she has a micro-chip. Mom's in Boston visiting Becky for a few days. The way things are going, she probably won't be back until next week. And I really don't want to take Joshua to the mall. Too much stimulation sends him into a meltdown and I don't think I can deal with that right now."

"I'll watch him."

I frown. "I can't leave him with you. You've never looked after him. You have no idea –. "

Sarah holds up a hand. "Give me one good reason why I can't babysit Joshua? I've watched other people's kids more than once, you know."

I lean forward and lock eyes with her. "Because… because he's not like other kids. He has autism."

There! I've said it.

"So?"

"So?" I snort. "You act as though it's nothing more than a simple cold."

"I'm sure we'll be fine, Abby. Trust me."

I stare at her, temporarily dumbstruck. I want to scream at her, to tell her about the meltdowns, the obsessions, the phobias, the irrational fears. Instead, I grab my cup and rise to pour the tea down the drain. The aroma is making me as nauseous as the conversation.

"Do you have any idea how difficult he can be?" I ask, my back to her.

Glancing out the kitchen window, I notice the woodpecker isn't in his usual tree. Perhaps he's wiser than me and has moved on.

"Stop worrying about what may or may not happen. It can't be that hard to watch him for a few hours."

"Autism is not as simple as you seem to think," I cry out, slamming my hand on the counter so hard the cup rattles in its saucer. "It's a constant struggle to make your child's world safe and less painful. It's a daily fight against fears, obsessions, and panic attacks. At any moment a noise or a smell can send him into a tailspin, triggering him to scream and bang his head against the floor or the walls to stop the assault on his overdeveloped senses. Most of the time it's a losing battle, like trying to hold water in your hand."

"I'm sorry," she says, softly. "I didn't know."

Sarah's words are like rain on a smoldering piece of coal. I wheel around to find her soft, green eyes are filled with concern. She truly cares. About me. About Joshua. About our future.

I shrug. "Okay. Fine. You can watch him for a couple of hours. Two hours ought to give you an idea whether you can handle him or not. Maybe they have an opening at Doo or Dye Hair Salon. I really need to do something about these awful highlights."

Sarah's eyes twinkle with amusement. "I was wondering whether you ran out of hair dye or you were starting a new trend."

Her giggle effectively douses the last embers of irritation lingering in my heart. I let out a little laugh. "I was dying my hair on Thursday, but Joshua had an incident and I had to stop."

"Go on, then. See what the stylists at the hair salon can do with that brassy hairdo. Joshua and I will be fine."

"If he gets out of hand –. "

She stands, then wraps an arm around my shoulders, gently propelling me towards the front door. "Joshua will be okay. He's like any other kid, only with a few more quirks. We'll figure it out."

"Hang on a second, I need to tell Joshua I'm leaving."

He's in the living room, watching the weather. "Joshua, Mommy's going out for a little bit. Sarah is going to stay with you."

His gaze is fixed on the TV. I crouch down so my face blocks the screen. "Joshua, did you hear me?"

Joshua grunts and pushes me away.

"Goodbye, Joshua."

My son doesn't even acknowledge my farewell. He's more interested in the weather than anything I might have to say.

"At least he doesn't suffer from separation anxiety," I say, giving a half-hearted laugh.

I stand and pick up my purse. "Be sure to secure all three locks behind me," I say, reaching for the door handle. "And call me on my cell if he's too much."

"We'll be fine," Sarah says. "Besides, I've always enjoyed a challenge."

I open the door, pause, then turn back. "I'm sorry. I just can't do this."

"Abby, I promise I will call you if he has a meltdown of Tsunami proportions. Otherwise, don't fret. Trust me, we'll be alright."

With those words, she gently pushes me out the door.

"Wait!" I turn back towards the house. But she'd already closed the door and engaged the locks.

I've just been kicked out of my own home.

CHAPTER SEVENTEEN

Driving to the hair salon, I'm as giddy as a child who's been let out of school early. No husband, no kid, no responsibilities for a couple of hours. Unfortunately, the euphoria soon mutates back into anxiety as I envision Joshua in meltdown mode. Will Sarah be able to handle him? She's watched me interact with him on several occasions and played with him for a few minutes while I fixed dinner or ran to the restroom. This, however, is totally different. Will she be able to read his body cues? Will she know how to cope with him when he's upset?

I glance at my phone, checking to make sure the battery is charged. I fully expect her to call within the first hour, frantic and crying for help. While I appreciate her offer, she has no clue what she's taking on. Perhaps she will understand my protective behavior a bit more after this.

Doo or Dye Hair Salon is one of several stores housed in a strip mall just five blocks from our house. Wedged between an office supply store to the left, and a wool shop advertising a going-out-of-business sale to the right, the salon doesn't possess much curb-appeal. The green awnings above each retail space could use a lick of paint and the sidewalk is cracked in several spots. What the place lacks in allure is clearly offset by Simon's reputation and skill. He owns the salon and his regular clients, like me, are not tempted by the recent boom of beauty salons popping up all over Springfield because Simon is undoubtedly the best coiffeur in town.

As I pull into a parking spot in front of the salon, I try to subdue a sudden case of nerves. I shut off the engine and sit back in the driver's seat, watching through the floor-to-ceiling windows as Simon trims a young girl's hair. Combing out one lock at a time, he pinches the strands between his index and middle finger, snips the ends, then combs them out again. His lips move as he chats with her, a smile lighting up his face each time his eyes meet hers in the mirror.

At the mani-pedi station, a young woman with spiky blond hair, probably in her early twenties, sits hunched over the hands of a middle-aged woman. The tip of her lip protrudes from between lips pierced by two golden hoops and bobs up and down as she concentrates on the manicure. She's never worked on my nails, but I've heard a lot of positive remarks about her. Rumor has it that she's Simon's younger sister. If she has half his talent, she'll drum up a lot more business for Doo or Dye.

Glancing at my nails, I let out a sigh. Before I had Joshua, I used to treat myself to weekly manicures. Now my nails look a mess, cut short so I don't accidentally scratch Joshua. I don't even bother with nail polish anymore because it seems so futile. My, how life has changed!

I reach for the door handle, then slump back as my phone rings. *That sure didn't take long!* Glancing at the screen, I'm relieved to see it's not her, just some stupid reminder from my carrier about privacy settings. But it gets me thinking what might happen if Sarah calls for help while I'm in the middle of a dye job. I can't just get up and leave. Then again, Sarah probably wouldn't call, even if Joshua erupted like Mount Vesuvius.

My mind sieves through my meager options. What if I buy the dye at the store, take it home and apply it myself while Sarah watches Joshua? That would probably be the smartest move. For several moments, I watch with envy as the two customers enjoy a few minutes' pampering. How I wish I could trade places with them for just one day! Simple pleasures mean so much when they are suddenly snatched away.

Sighing, I turn the key in the ignition, craning my neck to see as I back out of the parking space. It's a short drive to the drugstore, just two blocks away. I check my phone again as I park the car in front of the store. Nothing. I'm not sure whether to rejoice or be concerned.

"Think positive," I scold myself.

Shifting from of the coolness of my car to the sweltering heat outside sucks the air out of my lungs. The humidity is like a spider's web, sticky, cloying, suffocating, and impossible to shuck off. On the horizon, corrugated clouds undulate across the darkening sky. The scent of rain permeates the air, promising a storm before nightfall.

The store's big, sliding doors whoosh open, welcoming me into its cool embrace. Beach chairs, swim rings, inflatable toys and sunscreen are on display at the front of the store with large signs advertising up to eighty percent off while quantities last. For a second, I am tempted to purchase the red pail and shovel set for Joshua. Then I remember the yellow pail and shovel my parents bought him just a couple of months ago, which still lay in the trunk of my car. He never plays with them because he'd rather use his hands in the sand.

I grab one of the store's baskets and head for the beauty aisle. There are so many hair-care products, it's a bit overwhelming. Should I go back to my original hair color, dye it the same color as the highlights, or try a fresh look altogether? Picking a box off the shelf, I turn it over and glance at the instructions.

"May I help you?" A salesclerk walks towards me, a smile lighting up her face. Her small, oval face is framed by strait, copper-colored hair. Appropriately, her name tag reads *Ginger*.

Tugging on my ponytail, I show her my tangerine-orange streaks. "I started coloring some highlights into my hair on Thursday but was interrupted when my son –." I pause and think. "Well, let's just say he had an incident – he has autism," I add, as though that simple word explains it all.

"I see," Ginger says. "Then I would suggest a simple fix. This one is a favorite and doesn't take much time." She hands me a package of hair dye that appears close to my original hair color. I turn the box over and scan the instructions.

"Seems fairly easy." I smile at her. "Thank you."

Ginger smiles back. "I have a nephew with autism. I understand."

I grip the box as though it's a life ring. "Thank you."

I swallow as pressure builds up behind my eyes then quickly turn away so she won't see the tears.

Biting my upper lip helps staunch the tears. I certainly don't want to cause a scene. As I hurry towards the check-out line, I pass a display of home pregnancy tests. I pause, then grab the first kit on the shelf. Ironically, the box I chose depicts a smiling couple on the front. I wince and drop it into my basket.

"Well, if it isn't my lovely neighbor with the invisible dog!" My stomach pitches at the sound of Clara's shrill voice.

She shuffles down the aisle towards me, her steps slow and awkward as she leans on the cart for support. Her metal cane hangs on the handle.

Somehow I muster a smile. "Hello, Clara. What are you doing here?"

"I have a prescription to pick up," she says, her eyes darting to the shelves where I was standing seconds earlier. "Thinkin' ya might be havin' another one?"

My heart sinks. "No, no, I was picking up a kit for my friend. She's tied up at home and asked me to get her one while I was out."

"That so?" She squints at me with her beady little eyes. "It's not like ya need another one when yer constantly losing the one ya have."

I glare at her, wishing I could chase her away like my dad when he shoos the nasty, black crows from his crops. "I'll see you later, Clara."

"By the way," I hear Clara's voice following me down the aisle, "I still haven't seen that dog of yours."

Ignoring the old coot, I hightail it to the cash register, pay for my purchases and rush out into the oppressive heat.

CHAPTER EIGHTEEN

As soon as I step into the house, I'm struck by the sound of laughter. A jumble of thoughts and emotions assail me all at once; relief, jealousy, protectiveness, a sense of inadequacy. While I'm glad to hear my son enjoying himself, it bothers me that Sarah is the one who's coaxed the laughter out of him. I feel cheated. Laughter is an emotional response Joshua mostly keeps buried inside. It is a rare and precious gift when he deigns to share it with us.

I follow the giggles upstairs, wondering what's so funny. The laughter is coming from the bathroom where Martin's deep chuckle mingles with Sarah's melodic laugh and Joshua's more subdued giggle. Apparently, my husband returned while I was out.

My jaw drops as I pause in the doorway. Joshua and the dog are both in the tub, suds adorning their heads. Sarah kneels beside the tub, smiling, as Joshua scoops up another handful of bubbles and places them on the pup's head. Oddly enough, the pup doesn't seem to mind.

Martin is the first to notice me standing there slack-jawed. Pushing away from the wall, he grabs my arm and steers me into our bedroom, quietly closing the door behind us.

"I know what you're thinking, Abby," he begins.

I sink down on the end of the bed, still in shock. "Can you –."

Martin holds up a hand. "Abby, stop. Stop right there. I know you have this…this obsession about germs. But Sarah has accomplished what neither one of us could. Not only is Joshua in the tub, he's actually enjoying his bath. He even washed himself, including his hair, which is a monumental feat. As for the dog, you needn't worry. I had her groomed while we were at the vet."

"But – a dog –."

His eyes narrow. "When you step out of this room, you will not utter a single disparaging word about the dog being in the bath."

"But the dog –."

"Abby, let it go."

But I don't know how to let it go.

"Sarah deserves praise for what she's achieved, not criticism. Understood?" I've never heard him speak so firmly to me before.

I nod, unsure of what has happened. Numb with shock, I watch Martin turn and leave the room.

Grabbing his pillow, I throw it at his retreating back but he's already out the door. Part of me wants to cry, another part wants to storm out of the house. If he and Sarah are so competent, I might just as well leave them to finish what they've started. Maybe I'll go back to Doo or Dye after all.

Glancing at the plastic bag I'm still clutching, I set it on the bed, then take out the dye kit and pregnancy test. From the bathroom, sounds of water draining down the pipes announce bath time is over. I shudder at the thought of the dog shaking herself dry, splashing water and fur all over the bathroom. Of course, I'll be the one scrubbing it down later on.

A knock on the door startles me.

"Okay if I come in?" Sarah asks, sticking her head around the door.

I wave her in and Sarah plops down next to me. She glances at my hair. "You couldn't get in at Doo or Dye?"

I shake my head. "I figured it could take a while and wasn't comfortable leaving Joshua that long. So I stopped by the drugstore and bought a home kit. Figured I could do as good a job as Simon, as long as I don't get interrupted again."

Sarah must sense my sober tone. Wrapping an arm around my shoulder, she pulls me close. "You are an incredible mom, Abby. You always put

Joshua's welfare before your own. I wish my mom was like that, but she was always more interested in her career than raising her own daughter."

Sarah lets her arm drop and lowers her gaze. "I hope when I have kids I'm more like you than my mother."

In that moment, her words do more for me than any counseling ever could.

"Thanks. I needed to hear that," I say, blinking hard against the tears. "Sometimes I wonder."

Sarah's face scrunches up like she's bitten into a pickle. "Don't ever judge your abilities as a mother. You're a wonderful mom."

I'm speechless.

"By the way, Joshua spilled grape juice on himself, so I threw his clothes in the washing machine," Sarah says. "They're soaking in cold water for now."

"Thanks, Sarah. You're such a good friend," I say, patting her hand.

"Meanwhile, your hair still looks rather sad," she says, the corners of her eyes crinkling as she stifles a laugh. "Want me to stick around so you can dye your hair without interruption?"

I hesitate. "Would you mind? Or Martin can watch him now he's home."

"Tell you what. I'll stay till the dye has properly set,"

she answers. "Then Martin can take over from there. How does that sound?"

I chuckle. "Perfect!"

Sarah pushes herself off the bed. She pauses just inside the door. "See you in church tomorrow?"

"It's Martin's turn this week. We have to alternate because Joshua can't tolerate the noise and the crowds."

Sarah nods. "I understand. I'll call you sometime next week, then."

"Sounds great. Thanks again for spending time with Joshua."

"You're welcome," she says, closing the door gently behind her.

CHAPTER NINETEEN

Shoulders slumped, I stand at the window, watching as rain sluices down. A flash of lightning illuminates the dark sky, followed seconds later by a loud crash of thunder. Why does it have to rain now, after so many days of drought? It's as though the skies have conspired to thwart my plans to coerce the dog into sleeping outside.

"Obviously the puppy didn't have a microchip," I say, over my shoulder. "Does the vet have any suggestions for finding its owner?"

"Not really," Martin says from his recliner. He's watching some video about dog training. "He called a couple who recently lost their Lab but they weren't home. He left a message on their answering machine and promised he'd keep an ear out. In the meantime, she's ours."

I spin around. "You want to keep her, don't you?"

"Can't you see what she'd doing for Joshua?" Martin says, pausing the TV. He turns to look at me.

"For one thing, the two of them have already formed quite a bond. Joshua loves that dog more than anything and she loves him right back. For another, the dog seems to sense Joshua's moods. It's a bit eerie, but if you watch her closely, you'll notice she senses when Joshua's upset. She'll nudge him or distract him from whatever's troubling him. She's probably the best therapist he's ever had. Cheaper, too."

"Who's going to walk her, train her, feed her, and clean up after her?" I jab my chest. "Me, that's who. Don't you think I have enough on my plate right now, without having to take on another burden?"

Martin stands and walks over to me. Placing one hand on each arm, he looks into my eyes. "I promise I will do as much as I can to help. I'll train her, even if it means taking her to classes after work."

I snort. "With the hours you keep? Some days you don't get home until after supper. How are you going to find time for dog training when your work schedule is so unreliable?"

"I'm not sure yet," Martin replies. "But I will find a way because I am convinced that this dog is no random accident. I honestly believe she is the answer to our prayers." His voice softens. "For the first time in months, I feel hopeful again."

Tears gleam in his eyes. His emotion is palpable and real.

"Martin, I need to think about this. I need time."

"Abby, I know you're not crazy about pets, especially in the house. All I'm asking is that you give her a chance. Watch Joshua and the dog over the next couple of days. I know you'll see what I've witnessed for myself."

A clap of thunder makes me jump. This is going be a long and noisy night. Joshua is terrified of storms. He'll hide under the bed or squeeze into the closet. I'll be up, of course, waiting until the storm passes, then coax him out of his hiding place and back into bed.

"By the way, whose idea was it to put the dog in the tub, yours or Sarah's?"

"It wasn't like that, Abby. As soon as we got home, the dog went looking for Joshua. Sarah was trying to coax him into the tub because he'd spilled grape juice on himself. The dog saw the water and jumped in. Joshua was so tickled, he climbed in after her."

So, it wasn't planned. Sadly, it leaves me feeling a little bit better. Call it catty, but at this point, I don't like the thought that Sarah can handle Joshua better than me.

"Where is that dog, anyway?" I ask, glancing around the living-room.

"Genevieve is in bed, with Joshua," Martin says, his tone matter-of-fact.

A loud snort explodes through my nostrils. "Genevieve? You can't be serious! No one in their right mind would call a dog Genevieve."

"What? It's kind of cute; Joshua and Genevieve."

Hands to my face, I shake my head. The man has no taste.

"If you're thinking of kicking her out in that storm, then you can forget it," Martin says. "She has no place to shelter from the rain. Besides, now she's nice and clean so you don't have to obsess over fleas or dirt."

"But she can't –."

Martin places a finger over my lips. "Shhh!" he says, grabbing my hand as he leads me towards Joshua's room. "Come see."

I feel a little bit foolish, tiptoeing through my own home like a thief. When we reach Joshua's room, I peer in. The night-light provides just enough glow for me to see my little boy curled up in bed, snuggled tight against the dog. He's asleep, a smile on his face. Huddled beside him, the black Labrador sleeps peacefully. I could swear she's smiling too.

CHAPTER TWENTY

I wake to silence. Flipping over to check Martin's side of the bed, I see it's empty. The sheet is a crumpled heap where he's tossed it aside. I strain to hear voices but the only sound is my own breathing. Where are Martin and Joshua?

A wave of nausea hits me, fast and hard. Rushing to the bathroom, I lean over the toilet and vomit. As I lower myself to the floor, ready for the next round, I remember the pregnancy kit I hid in the drawer under the sink. Hands shaking, I unwrap the package, praying it turns out negative, then suffer a pang of guilt for thinking that way.

But I'm not ready for another challenge. I just can't manage a second child right now. Joshua takes up most of my time, day and night. How can I care for two little ones when I'm barely coping now? How will I survive with even less sleep? A baby will simply complicate matters. Worse yet, can I find it in me to lavish this child with the love he or she deserves?

The realization that I slept through the night for the first time in months suddenly hits me. Did Joshua stay in bed all night or was I simply too tired to hear him?

I run the test, place the stick on the tank cover, then wander into the bedroom to change into some comfy sweats. As I pull them from the chest of drawers, my eyes fall on the latest issue of *Fashion Sense* resting on the dresser. A young, sexy woman smiles from the front cover. Her make-up is perfect, her hair flawless, and her outfit is to die for.

Flipping through the pages, I pause as a full-page ad catches my interest. In the photo, a little girl watches her mother apply lipstick in front of the mirror. Bold letters state, "Not your mother's lipstick." A sudden childhood memory jumps to mind of the day when Becky and I decided to play hide and seek while Mom was on the phone.

"You hide first," my sister said, covering her eyes. "One… two… three…."

Giggling with excitement, I ran upstairs to my parents' room and slipped into Mom's walk-in closet. Huddled on the floor, I waited for my sister to whip open the door and yell, "found you!"

When Becky didn't show up after a couple of minutes, I flipped on the closet light. Mom's closet was Aladdin's cave, bursting with all sorts of treasures; chunky gold necklaces, large hoop earrings, glitzy costume jewelry, beaded clutch-purses, oversized shoulder bags, colorful scarves, and shoes in every color imaginable.

Dragging a bright yellow purse from one of the shelves, I zipped it open and peeked inside. There, amid wads of Kleenexes and chewing-gum wrappers, lay a tube of cherry-red lipstick. To a three-year old, lipstick is magic on a stick.

Clutching my treasure in one hand, I opened the closet door and peered out; no one in sight. Slipping quietly out of the closet, I tiptoed past the banister, pausing to listen. I could hear Mother's soft voice downstairs, talking to someone on the other end of the line, and cabinet doors opening and closing as my sister continued her search. Stifling a giggle, I hurried into the bathroom and shut the door.

Dragging a stepstool over to the sink, I climbed up so I could see myself in the mirror. Carefully, I removed the cap, then puckered my lips as I'd seen mother do. I was pressing the lipstick to my lips when my sister burst in.

"Found you!" she'd yelled.

Startled, my hand jerked, smearing a blood-red streak across my right cheek.

Becky's jaw dropped. "You are soooo in trouble!"

Snatching a tissue from the tissue box, I frantically tried to scrub away the smudge. But I only made it worse.

"Oh no!" I said, looking to my sister for help.

She wasn't even paying attention to me. Instead, she was eyeing the tube of lipstick. With the speed of a striking cobra, she snatched it up and ran it over her lips.

"Pretty!" I said, staring at my sister's gorgeous red lips. "Pretty!"

Becky started laughing. Soon, I was laughing too. We were laughing so hard, we never heard Mom coming until her petite but mighty frame filled the doorway. Mother wasn't especially tall but, standing there, arms on her hips and a you-are-in-big-trouble look in her eyes, she appeared rather formidable.

I laugh at the memory. That incident was the first of several that prompted me to become a beautician. I was well on my way to obtaining an associate degree in cosmetology when Joshua was born. At first, I thought I would take a short break, then resume my training after Joshua started pre-school. But those plans had to be placed on hold because of Joshua's autism. Suddenly, that dream seems like a dreadful joke that exploded in my face.

Anger surges within me; anger at the wicked trick life has played on me, anger at my own helplessness and deep disappointment. Anger at the wicked thief called autism. Flinging the magazine across the room, I burst into tears. I cry for lost dreams. I cry for Joshua and the fiend from which he cannot escape. I cry for the plans Martin and I made, which appear so unfeasible now. I cry for the future which is unclear and out-of-control. I cry until there are no more tears to shed.

Overwhelmed by emotion, I sweep my hand across the vanity table, sending mascara, eye liner, foundation, lipstick, jewelry, and lotions tumbling to the ground. Dropping to the floor, I sob my heart out. I can't do this anymore. I can't continue living life as it is. I need help. Joshua needs help. Desperately.

CHAPTER TWENTY-ONE

"**A**bby! Are you okay?" Martin stands just inside the door, eyes darting about as he takes in the chaos. "I was out back with Joshua and the dog when I heard a crash."

."No, Martin, I'm not okay," I say, glancing up at him.

I want him to come and hold me, console me. Instead, he picks up items, one by one, cleaning up the mess I've made. I wait as he makes his way to the bathroom, dumping the items he's collected onto the vanity table. He steps into the bathroom and turns on the faucet to wash his hands.

The water shuts off, then silence. Seconds later, Martin's large form looms in the doorway. He's holding the pregnancy test between his thumb and forefinger.

"What's this?" he asks, quietly.

"Exactly what it looks like, Martin," I snap. "It's positive, isn't it?"

Martin nods, and I start crying all over again. This time, Martin sits down beside me and pulls me into his arms.

"I – can't – do this – any – more." My words come out garbled against his chest.

"But this is wonderful, honey. We're going to have a baby!"

I pull away and stare at him as if he's insane. "You can't be serious. I need another baby like I need a hole in the head. I can barely cope with one child, let alone two."

"Maybe this baby will help draw Joshua out of his own little world?" Martin suggests.

"Or push him even further in."

"This could also give you something new to focus on other than Joshua's erratic behaviors. Maybe it will help you get over Joshua's autism."

"I don't want to get over Joshua's autism," I yell. "I want to fix it. I want answers. I want my little boy back."

Martin's jaw twitches. He appears to be at a loss for words. "So – so you don't want this baby?"

I feel an urge to scream. "You can be so dense at times. Have you ever considered the possibility this baby might have autism too?"

There's a beat of silence. I can tell my words have shaken him. He staggers to his feet, tossing the test stick into the trash.

"Joshua's autism has really affected you, hasn't it?" The usual warmth is missing from his voice.

Walking to the door, he pauses in the doorway. "Just be careful you don't let what you want blind you to all the blessings you have."

Watching him leave, I feel as though I've deeply disappointed him. I mull over Martin's words as they spool through my mind in a continuous loop. *Don't let what you want blind you to all the blessings you have.* Has finding a way to 'fix' my child become my sole focus, to the exclusion of everything and everyone else? Does Martin feel like I'm neglecting him? Would he leave me if he thought Joshua's autism mattered more than our marriage? What does our future look like? I shudder to think of the possibilities.

Maybe he's right. Maybe it's time to exchange my hopes and dreams for a different size before there's nothing left but tattered rags.

CHAPTER TWENTY-TWO

"Don't forget to stop at the pet store on your way home from church," I call out as Martin grabs his keys on his way out.

He's been very quiet and withdrawn since our talk. Asking him to buy a doghouse so the pup can sleep outside has only exacerbated his sulky mood.

The fact that I slept through the night for the first time in months is not lost on me. Yet I'm reluctant to admit it's due to the dog. Even though Martin thinks it's okay for the dog to sleep with Joshua, I'm still resisting it. I can't wrap my mind around the idea of a dog sharing my son's bed, not yet at least. I need more proof that the dog actually is helping him.

To me it seems so coincidental. But that's the irony of living with autism. Even though I desperately want healing for my child, I've grown skeptical. We've tried so many treatments, diets, medications, and therapies that promised to bring breakthroughs, yet failed to make the slightest difference, that now I need to be convinced, beyond the shadow of a doubt, that there's an undeniable correlation between the dog's presence and Joshua's change in behavior. I need to see for myself that Martin's claims aren't merely a ploy to convince me we should keep the dog.

"Want to watch the weather while Mommy gets dressed?" I ask Joshua.

Although it's part of his daily routine, I continue to ask, hoping for a nod or even better, a "yes, Mommy." Two simple words, yet my four-year-old still can't or won't utter them. Sometimes I wonder if we've forgotten to flip on a switch in his brain. If only it were that simple!

I turn on the TV, watching as Joshua settles himself on the floor with the dog snuggled up against him. I've noticed Joshua doesn't jump or wave his arms in front of the television as much since she's been here. It's obvious he enjoys her company. But is that reason enough to keep her?

I sigh and head upstairs. In the bathroom, I grab a washcloth, run it under the faucet, then bring the warm, wet cloth up to my face. The woman in the mirror scowlsg back at me, dark circles under her pained, blue eyes. Slowly, I raise the washcloth to my face to hide this disturbing reflection. When did I grow so surly and cynical?

I close my eyes, then scrub my face vigorously with the washcloth. I tie my now-blond hair into a ponytail, then apply a bit of foundation and concealer to help mask my sickly look.

"What you see is what you get," I grumble.

The scrape of wood against bare floors catches my ear. What's my son up to now?

"Joshua, what are you doing?" I ask, charging into the kitchen.

One of the kitchen chairs is positioned beneath the cabinet where I keep the cookies, Joshua right beside it.

"Do you want a cookie? I ask, frowning.

Joshua grunts and points.

"If you want a cookie, you need to ask. You know Mommy doesn't like you climbing on chairs."

Joshua begins to shuffle his feet.

I try to lock eyes with him. "If you want a cookie, then say 'cookie'."

Although elective mutism is part of his autism and stems from anxiety, his speech therapist has encouraged us to hold out as long as we can in hopes it will push him to speak. But pressing the matter only increases his anxiety level, so I struggle with the choice of forcing the issue, or letting it pass in order to avoid a meltdown. Neither option appeals to me.

I decide to give it one more try. "Joshua, say 'cookie.'"

Joshua drops to the floor, fussing as he kicks his feet against the cupboards.

"Joshua, stop!"

I'm about to grab Joshua before he hurts himself when the dog bounds into the kitchen, whining loudly. Tail between her legs, she whimpers and nudges Joshua's face. Speechless, I watch as Joshua falters, then wraps his arms around her, pulling her close. My chest tightens. I can't breathe.

Abruptly, Joshua pushes the dog away, stands up and strolls out of the kitchen as though nothing happened. The dog scampers after him, tail wagging as she follows him into the living room. A bark of laughter catches in my throat. I can't believe what I've just witnessed. That dog has accomplished in seconds a feat Martin and I have been trying to achieve for over three years.

Now I finally understand what Martin meant when he said he was feeling hopeful again. That same sense of hope begins to stir within me.

"Maybe Martin is right," I whisper. "Perhaps she was meant for us all along."

Who would have thought an animal could do more for Joshua than his own parents or therapists? On the other hand, nothing to do with his condition has made much sense. The dog is simply another mystery I add to the long list of unanswered questions in Joshua's journey with autism.

CHAPTER TWENTY-THREE

"Is this the Raynes residence?"

When the phone rang, I assumed it was Mom calling to tell me Becky had gone into labor. I certainly wasn't expecting to hear a thick, gravelly voice on the other end of the line.

"Who's calling?"

"My name is Butch. Got a call last night from our vet saying you found a black Lab. I was hoping to stop by this morning to see if it's ours."

My heart clenches. Just yesterday, I was hoping we would find the dog's owner. Now I wonder what will happen if Joshua has to part with her.

"Can you describe the dog?" I ask, wanting to be sure this person is legit.

"She's a black Labrador, about ten months old."

"Sounds about right," I answer.

"I could come by in a few minutes, if you'll give me your address."

"Actually, we were on our way out," Not quite true, but I'm leery about giving out our address to strangers, especially with Martin away. "Why don't I swing by your house?"

"Sure. Whatever."

I jot down his address then hang up, a tangle of emotions roiling inside me like thunderclouds. In the living-room, Joshua and the puppy lay side by side, looking at a book about rain clouds.

"Come, Joshua. It's a nice day. Let's go for a ride." I feel like a traitor and wish I didn't have to bring him along. This is going to break his little heart.

Stepping outside is like walking into a sauna. Last night's rain has brought no relief from the blistering heat. Instead, the humidity feels like as heavy and oppressive as the weight tugging at my heart.

Across the street the lace curtains part. I wave at Clara, smiling as I tug gently on the dog's leash so she's in plain view. Opening the car door, I usher Joshua and the Lab into the back seat, then glance at Clara's house once more. She's left her post.

The address Butch provided is on the other side of town, in a neighborhood I've never driven through. Bags of litter squat on the curb, waiting for garbage day. Flimsy wire fences dissect the narrow properties on which crouch tiny houses, most of them in need of a fresh coat of paint and some basic repairs. Butch's house hunkers between a boarded-up house with blackened windows, and a vacant lot where two bare-chested teenagers lean against a brown Oldsmobile propped on cinder blocks, laughing and sharing a smoke.

"Stay in the car," I tell Joshua as I climb out and venture up three rickety steps to the front porch.

I finger the canister of pepper spray in my pocket as I knock on the door. Out back, a frenzy of furious barking and snarling erupts as several dogs fling themselves against a chain-link fence. My chest tightens and suddenly I find myself wishing I'd worn my sneakers instead of wedged sandals.

"Shut up!" a lusty voice booms inside the house.

Instantly, the cacophony ceases. I grip my pepper spray a little tighter.

"Mrs. Raynes?" A beefy man asks, through the screen door. He looks like the kind of guy who tips tractor tires over and over just for fun. Dark smudges stain his large hands and his grubby T-shirt is streaked with black smudges. He smells of engine oil.

"That's right," I nod, glancing back at my Impala. I wish I'd waited for Martin to come with me. Not my best decision, by far.

"Where's the mutt?" he asks, pushing open the screen door. His eyes are cold as steel as he looks down at me.

"In the car. I thought it best to leave her there until I was sure I had the right address."

He pushes past me, then stomps down the wooden stairs.

"Just a sec'," I yell, hustling to catch up with him. "My son is in the car and I won't have you scaring him."

"Butch!" a female voice yells from the porch.

Glancing over my shoulder, I spot an anorexic-looking woman stepping out of the house. Her hair is streaked with grey, and the sleeves on her threadbare housedress are too short to hide the bruise marks on the inside of each arm. "Let the lady get the dog out."

Butch stops beside the car and peers inside.

"Could you step back, please?" My voice is strong and authoritative, even though my legs are like jelly. Mom-zilla is back.

He steps aside so I can open the rear door. The puppy leans into Joshua, her eyes wide and fearful. She's trembling so hard it tears at my heart.

"You know, I think we made a mistake. When did you say you lost your dog?"

Butch frowns. "Couple days ago."

He leans into the car to get a better look. A shriek explodes from the back seat as Joshua dissolves into a meltdown. One arm is wrapped around the dog, the other one is scratching at his face. His eyes are wide with terror as he screams and screams.

Butch backs away, eyes wide, drops of sweat beading on his forehead. "What's wrong with him?"

"He has autism," I snap. "And you just scared the living daylights out of him."

Behind me, the woman snorts. "No such thing as autism. My niece has a kid like him. Just needs a firm hand and a mother who can make him understand who's boss."

Blood rushes to my face and I have to bite my lips to stop myself from getting in her face and screaming at her.

"I'm sorry, but this was a mistake. This dog has been with us for several weeks." I know I've told another fib, but I can't bear to surrender Joshua's puppy to people who will mistreat her. Sometimes you have to choose between the lesser of two evils.

I slam the rear door shut, climb into the driver's seat, and throw the car into reverse. Tires squealing, I back out of the driveway, whip the steering wheel into a sharp left turn, then stomp on the gas. I don't even look back.

My heart thumps so hard, it hurts. It feels like a steel-drum band is pounding away in my chest. In the back seat, Joshua sobs, his face buried in the dog's neck. Both of his arms are wrapped tightly around the dog as she nuzzles her head into Joshua's chest. I despise myself for submitting my son to such a terrible situation. What was I thinking? How could I even consider taking away the one thing which gives him so much joy?

"It's okay, Joshua," I say, my voice shaky. "Everyone's going to be fine. Let's go home now and get ready to go to Grandpa's."

The crying subsides just a tad. I suck in a deep breath. I guess the dog is ours now.

CHAPTER TWENTY-FOUR

I always enjoy our Sunday jaunts to the country. Like an oasis in the desert, my childhood home provides a respite from the clamor of city life. For a few hours, I can escape the chaos of autism and enjoy simple pleasures such as leisurely strolls, adult conversation, and Mom's homemade apple pie.

Joshua is also much happier at the farm. It's as if he's one with nature, free to run and jump and howl without censure. His voice melds with the bleats and squawks of the birds and animals, a language uninhibited by rules or structure.

It's a beautiful drive from our house to my parents' farm. As soon as we leave the highway, we find ourselves on narrow, dirt roads snaking through luscious, green farmland dotted with Angus, Hereford, and Longhorn cows. In the fields, round bales of hay bake in the sultry summer heat, reminding me of Mom's giant fluffy cinnamon rolls, oozing with butter, brown sugar, cinnamon, and ground pecans.

Above us, a lone falcon soars on the breeze, its shrill cry piercing the noonday silence. A few puffy clouds waft lazily across a clear blue sky, like sailboats drifting on a smooth lake. It promises to be a good afternoon.

My shoulders relax and my breathing slows as the peaceful scenery shears away some of the stress I've been carrying for the past several days. Closing my eyes, I inhale deeply, savoring this rare moment of serenity.

In the backseat, Joshua is sound asleep. He looks adorable in his bib overalls and barn-red rubber boots. Beside him, the dog sits erect, nose pressed against the window. This morning's encounter with Butch springs to mind and I wonder how such a sweet dog survived such terrible conditions. I guess we've helped her as much as she's helped our son. I close my eyes and breathe a prayer of thanks.

The sound of tires crunching on gravel wakes me. I must have fallen asleep while praying. To our left and right, green pastures spread out for miles, nudging up against the tree-covered hills undulating across the horizon like a row of men hunched over their work. A white-tailed doe stops her grazing, ears cupped forward, tail erect, soft, brown eyes watching our approach. Beside her, a fawn nibbles at the tender grass. In a blink, they're gone, bounding off across the field and into the woods where they can hide among the colorful mosaic of leaves.

The drive bends to the right and there, before us, stands my childhood home; a white, two-story farmhouse with a wrap-around porch where Mom and I have spent countless hours chatting about school, fashion, beauty tips, the complexity of boys, and the purpose of life. On summer evenings, we'd rock in our high-backed rocking chairs and listen to the serenade of cicadas, crickets, and bullfrogs, as they rendered their last ode to the waning summer day.

"We're here," I say over my shoulder.

Joshua stirs, then breaks into a smile when he spots Grandpa's farm. He loves it here, content to shadow his grandpa as he goes about his chores. The animals seem to sense Joshua is special, allowing him to pet them as if he were Grandpa himself. Even the old rooster who struts about like he owns the place and pecks anyone who comes too close, watches over Joshua from his perch atop the carcass of Dad's rusty red tractor.

I remember watching Dad as a child, astride the metal beast, sitting tall and straight as he headed out to the fields each morning, a thin ribbon of crimson barely visible on the eastern horizon. Like a fierce bull, the mechanical brute snorted and bucked, kicking up clouds of dust as my hero in denim overalls coaxed it onward once more.

I've barely opened the car door when Joshua and his dog tumble out and dash across the yard.

"Martin!" I yell. "Watch that dog!

Martin shrugs it off. "She's just gone to investigate."

"She won't come to any harm." My dad's deep baritone greets me from the porch. He's wearing jeans, his favorite Johnny Cash T-shirt, which Mom won't let him wear out in public, and scuffed up boots. I can't help but notice his mop of unruly grey hair needs a trim and his strong jaw sports several days' stubble. But he looks happy, like a kid playing hooky in order to go fishing.

"It's not her I'm worried about as much as Sally and Winchester," I say, watching Dad's two Australian Shepherds. Cautiously, the Shepherds assess their visitor, circling and sniffing, their tails slowly sweeping the air.

"Bah, they can fend for themselves," Dad says, wrapping me in a bear hug.

His strong embrace is like a ray of sun on a cold, gloomy day. His familiar scent of Folgers and fresh-cut hay welcome me home.

"How you doin', honey?"

"I'm okay, Dad. How about you?"

"Not bad, considering Mom checks on me every couple hours." His laugh is loud and contagious, and I can't help but smile. "When did you guys get a dog?"

I step away and glance at the pup. "We didn't. She's a stray that wouldn't take 'no' for an answer."

I'm tempted to tell him about our experience this morning, but I'm too ashamed to admit what a fool I was. "Joshua has grown attached to her already."

Dad opens his mouth, as if to speak, then stops. I follow his gaze. He's observing Joshua. Right now, my son looks like any other four-year old as he runs after the dog.

Dad rubs his chin. "She could be the best –."

"Hold that thought, Dad," I blurt, my stomach roiling as the smell of fresh horse droppings reaches my nostrils.

Covering my mouth with my hand, I push past him and make a mad dash for the house, barely making it to the bathroom in time.

After throwing up several times, I walk out of the bathroom to hear Dad's deep baritone resonating through the house. "To the new baby!"

I wince, wishing Martin hadn't spilled the news yet.

"To the new baby!" Martin echoes.

167

The clink of glasses tells me they're already toasting this child in my womb.

"Dad, please don't say anything to Mom," I say, sauntering into the kitchen. "It's early days and I'd rather keep it under wraps for now."

"But honey, this is wonderful news," my dad says, a broad smile spreading across his weathered face. "You know I can't keep secrets from your mother. She'll know something's up the minute she walks through the door."

I sigh. Unfortunately, he's right. Mom can sense any shift in family dynamics. Expecting Dad to keep a secret from her is like asking the sun not to shine. It isn't going to happen.

"Where's Joshua?" I ask.

Both of them give me blank looks.

"Two grown men and not one of them can keep an eye on a four-year-old," I grumble, throwing my hands in the air. "If Mom were here, she'd give both of you an earful."

Hurrying outdoors to find my son, I'm quickly overwhelmed by the smell of manure. I race back inside.

"Martin, go find Joshua!" I yell, sprinting for the bathroom.

So much for a quiet afternoon in the country.

CHAPTER TWENTY-FIVE

Between the nausea and the headache that's been lingering for the past couple of days, I'm completely wrung out. Martin and Dad have promised to watch Joshua while I lay down for a bit. I'm holding them to it.

Walking into my childhood bedroom is like stepping back in time. Not much has changed since the days when Becky and I shared this room. This was our sanctuary, our safe haven where we could share our hopes and dreams. Each night, after we'd exchanged our goodnights and Mom turned out the light, my sister and I would whisper secrets, emboldened by the concealment of darkness.

Today, the room is hot and stuffy with sunlight pouring in. I crank open one of the windows just a tad to let in a breeze. Outside, Joshua squeals with delight. He's riding Maggie the mare, clinging tightly to her thick black mane as Dad leads her slowly around the corral. Joshua loves Maggie, who always keeps an easy lope when he's in the saddle.

I lay down on the salmon-colored bedspread which covers my twin bed. Becky's is identical, two bedspreads cut from the same cloth. On the night-table between our beds is a framed photo of my sister and me hugging and smiling in front of the Christmas tree. I pick up the photo and study it. We both look so happy and innocent, my sister eight years old and me barely six. I can't help but wonder how two sisters who shared the same childhood could wind up with such different lives.

There was a time when I was sure of myself and my future. Back then, the hardest decision was what to wear and how to fix my hair. I didn't even question the probability that I would get married, have two perfect kids, start my own business and live happily-ever-after. Oh, the innocence of youth!

Then there's Becky, with her handsome husband, her successful career, and her first baby on the way. Some days I wish I could trade places with her. Life looks so promising for her, while mine is gradually falling apart.

I slam the photo face-down on the night table, angry at myself for making the comparison. A touch of guilt for entertaining such thoughts provokes me to tears. I swipe at my eyes, annoyed with these unwanted emotions. Enough with the pity party. I need to focus on my blessings and stop wishing for what isn't mine.

A soft knock on the door startles me. It's Martin.

"You should see Joshua riding on Maggie," he says, smiling. "A few more rides around the corral and we'll have ourselves a real cowboy."

His hazel eyes crinkle with humor, but I'm not in the mood for his jokes. When I don't respond, his smile falters.

"How's the nausea?"

"Better." I can't bring myself to look at him. He deserves so much more than I have to offer.

"Are you still worried about the baby?" He's pussyfooting around a touchy subject, knowing it's a potential minefield.

I nod.

"Let's not dwell on something that may never happen. Worrying can't change a thing. Just let it go."

I want to shout at him and pound his chest. Instead, I bite my lip and turn away. There was a time when his confident and easy-going temperament appealed to me. I loved the fact that he wasn't easily rattled, even when the tire on his Ford Explorer went flat on our first date and we had to trudge ten miles through a downpour because he didn't have a spare.

Yet now it's that laissez-faire attitude which rubs me the wrong way. Even though he loves me, and loves Joshua, he takes more of a "let's wait and see" attitude towards life, so contrary to my own obsession with fixing the status quo.

I struggle to keep my voice calm, despite the frustration welling up inside. "How, Martin? How do I let it go when you and I both know there's a chance he or she will also have autism?"

Gently, tenderly, Martin brushes the hair off my forehead. He's quiet for a moment, trying to measure his words. "Do you truly believe that?"

"I don't know what I believe anymore," I whisper, tears trickling down my cheeks.

A gentle breeze blows through the room, carrying with it snatches of laughter. At least someone is enjoying this day.

"One thing you can know for sure is that I love you and I'll always be there for you," Martin says. "We'll muddle through this together, somehow."

Martin removes my sandals then gently rubs my feet as I close my eyes and relax. He's my anchor in the storm, the one constant in times of trouble. Comforted by his reassurances, I finally slip into a restful sleep.

CHAPTER TWENTY-SIX

The rooster crows, disrupting my sleep. It's a wonder Mom hasn't turned him into Coq au Vin by now. Rubbing the sleep from my eyes, I sit up and listen for voices but the house is silent. Other than the faint chant of a whippoorwill, and the distant lowing of some cow, the place is quiet. The noisy world I usually inhabit has quelled its ceaseless babble for a while. I linger in its peaceful bosom, like a sated baby in its mother's arms.

Downstairs, Mom's Cuckoo clock sounds five o'clock. Reluctantly, I rise and shuffle to the window. The yard is empty, except for a few chickens scraping at the dirt, searching for bugs. Out in the distance, Dad's new tractor trundles across the fields. He must be giving Joshua a ride.

I wander down the stairs in stocking feet, skidding a tad on one of the newly-waxed steps and smile as I remember the time Becky and I took the stairs on our plastic toboggans. When Mom found out, she set us both to work, re-waxing the stairs until they shone.

As a child, I loved to slip and slide across the slick wooden floors. Sometimes I was a figure-skater, performing in front of a large crowd. Other times, I was a ballerina, resplendent in a pink tutu and silver tiara. Occasionally, Dad would snag me on his way to the kitchen and spin me around and around like a weathervane caught in a whirlwind.

Roaming through the house, I tidy and pick up as I go. I remove a wrench from the mahogany coffee table, a work shirt off the back of Mom's Lazy-Boy, a can of Mountain Dew from an end-table and return the remote that's on the couch to the TV stand. Mom would have a fit if she saw the house in such a state.

In the den, Martin sprawls on the sofa, watching a game between the St. Louis Cardinals and the Seattle Mariners. I love this room, with its rustic bookcases, the solid oak desk Dad built from our black walnut trees, the hunting trophies proudly displayed along the walls, and the worn leather couch Mom wanted to toss out when Becky and I accidentally burned holes in some of the cushions testing a new electric hair curler on each other. When Mom asked Dad to help her lug it out to the burn pile, he argued the couch had too much character and too many memories. So Mom banished it to Dad's den and replaced it with a stuffy French sofa made of grey cotton twill and no give.

"Want some popcorn?" Martin asks, holding up a large plastic bowl.

I wrinkle my nose and shake my head. "I see Dad is out, showing off his new tractor to Joshua."

Martin chuckles. "You'd think he'd given birth to the thing, the way he brags about it."

"I guess that's why he calls it his 'baby'. Speaking of which, we need to feed ours so we can head home soon. Could you help me fix supper? I doubt Dad has thought that far."

The kitchen has a different aura without Mom. Like a child neglected for too long, it clamors for some attention. Dishes are piled next to the sink and the counters are sticky to the touch. Newspapers, mail, and dozens of sticky notes – Mom's reminders to Dad - litter the large walnut table he made to celebrate their tenth wedding anniversary.

"You work on supper, I'll tackle the mess," I say, scrubbing the dark granite countertops while Martin checks what's in the fridge.

"How about an omelet? There's ham, a shelf full of eggs, some peppers, and several types of cheese."

"Let me wash a frying pan and we're in business."

I'm in the process of stowing the last of the plates in the dishwasher when a cloud of dust arises outside the window, announcing Dad's return. The tractor chugs into the yard, three dogs bringing up the rear, tongues dangling out the sides of their mouths.

The cab door opens and Joshua spills out. He's beaming.

"Why do we bother with therapy when we could bring Joshua to visit Dad every day?" I say, turning to Martin. "Those two have something special going on."

Martin nods. "They sure do."

Like a jackrabbit with a coyote on its heels, Joshua bolts across the yard and bursts into the house, his pup bounding along behind him.

"Hey, hey, put that dog outside," I yell, reaching to grab her collar as she darts past me.

I want to kick myself the moment the words leave my mouth. Joshua's lower lip quivers as Martin nabs the dog and pushes her out onto the deck. Joshua hits himself in the face with his fists then runs off. I struggle to breathe, as though the wind has been knocked out of me.

"Did you guys see Joshua driving that big, ole' tractor?" Dad's booming voice fills the kitchen as he walks in. He has no idea what's just happened.

176

"Before you know it, he'll be plowing and harvesting right alongside his grandpa."

I turn away so Dad won't notice my tears.

"Looked like you guys were having fun," Martin chuckles. He's covering for me, giving me time to gather myself.

The shrill ring of the phone rattles me. I snatch the receiver on the second ring. "Hello?"

"Becky had her baby!" Mom's voice is filled with excitement. "She's absolutely beautiful!"

"How much does the baby weigh?" I ask, glancing up. Martin and Dad are fist bumping.

"Six pounds, three ounces. With a headful of dark hair. I'll send you a picture as soon as I figure out how to use this smart phone."

"How's Becky?"

"Tired but doing very well. She's been moved to a post-partum room and Kevin is with her and the baby. I thought I'd give them a bit of privacy while I made a few phone calls. How's Dad doing?"

"Dad's fine. You can stop worrying about him. He took Joshua out on his new tractor this afternoon. Want to speak to him?"

"Sure. Put him on."

I hand the phone to Dad and go in search of Joshua, frustrated with my stupid reaction when the dog ran into the house. I need to unlearn this reactive behavior, to change the way I respond to negative situations. I need to think before I act.

"Joshua!" I call. "Time for dinner."

He's in the living-room, curled up in the yellow smiley-face beanbag Grandma made for him. His look is vacant. He's retreated back into the safety of his own little world.

Sitting on the floor, I lean on the edge of the beanbag. "Did you have fun riding on Grandpa's tractor?"

He remains silent, staring into space, ignoring my presence. I stoop to his level, try to lock eyes, willing him to come back though the sheer force of my love for him.

"I'm sorry about the dog."

No response.

"You know she's happy to be outside, playing with Grandpa's dogs?"

I could be talking to a stone, for all the feedback I'm getting. I press on, because I need to explain my reaction.

"Can I tell you a true story, Joshua?"

He stares at the floor, silent and unresponsive.

"When I was a little girl, about your age, I had a special friend named Hannah. She came to visit me one day and we thought it would be fun to have a tea party on the front porch. At the time, we had a dog named *Pooch*. Isn't that a funny name?"

I'm not sure if he's listening or understands, but I need to revisit this memory I've tucked away for so long.

"While Hannah and I drank our tea and sandwiches, Pooch joined us on the porch with a deer leg he'd found out in the woods."

I pause as the memories flood back. "Hannah needed to use the bathroom, so she ran inside. Pooch darted over, ate her sandwich in one gulp, then licked the crumbs off her plate. I remembered Mommy saying that dogs can carry harmful diseases, so I ran inside to fetch her a new plate without taking the dirty one in with me. While I was inside, Hannah went back out to the porch and helped herself to some chocolate-dipped strawberries. When I came out, she was already eating them off the plate Pooch had licked."

I take a breath. "A few minutes later, Hannah got very sick. She was so sick Grandma and Grandpa had to call an ambulance to take her to the hospital. Her parents told us later that she almost died. If only I had taken that dirty plate in with me after Pooch licked it, she wouldn't have been so sick."

A rush of pain rises in my throat and settles there.

"Is that what you've believed all these years?" Dad's voice startles me.

He crosses the room, a deep frown on his face. The muscles in his jaw twitch. "Pooch had nothing to do with Hannah's illness."

A jolt of shock racks my body. "He didn't?"

"Hannah had an allergic reaction to the strawberries. It was nobody's fault, no one knew about her allergy, not even her mother."

"Why…. Why didn't you tell me?" I ask, rising to my feet.

"We thought you knew."

My legs shake uncontrollably as I sit down on the couch. The sheer force of this revelation makes me want to yell, scream, laugh, and cry, all at the same time. All these years, I've been obsessing about germs because of what happened to Hannah, when all along it had nothing to do with Pooch. All at once, the remorse that has dogged me for so many years vanishes. I've finally been acquitted.

Pooch and me both.

CHAPTER TWENTY-SEVEN

The first star glitters in the night sky as we drive home.

"Joshua, look!" I say, pointing. "See the star?"

I turn to look at my son in the backseat. We've only been in the car for about three minutes, and already he is asleep. The dog's head rests in his lap. She too is sleeping.

Sitting back in my seat, I let out a sigh of contentment. Even though the nausea spoiled it a little, this day has provided a great deal of emotional healing. My conscience is lighter and the concern I'd been subconsciously nursing over Becky and her baby has eased.

"She sure is a beautiful baby," I say, glancing at the picture Mom sent to my smart phone.

Julie's tiny fists are curled beneath her chin, as though she's ready to take on the world. Her face, so delicate and perfect, reminds me of a pixie. I want to hold her, to breathe in her sweet baby scent, and sense that surge of love that comes with the precious gift of life.

A whisper of optimism flutters in my chest as I think about this child in my womb. I allow it to linger barely long enough to take root. Maybe she will be as beautiful and healthy as Julie. As long as I keep my heart open, there is room for hope.

"I wonder if Mom and Dad would watch Joshua for two or three days while I fly out to visit Becky and the new baby?" I say.

This would be a first. I briefly wonder if I can actually follow through with the idea.

Martin clears his throat. "About that."

I don't like the serious look on his face. "I've been taking a look at our funds. Our savings account is nearly wiped out, which means we're going to have to watch our spending habits if we choose to continue Joshua's therapies. Because our insurance doesn't cover autism services, we end up spending fifteen hundred dollars a month just for the therapy sessions. That means we'll either have to take out a second mortgage or I'll have to find a second job"

I squeeze my eyes shut as my heart plummets. Why does life have to be so hard? Just when I start thinking a little more positively about the future, life sucks me down again. Is there no end to these constant emotional upheavals?

"I could ask my parents for a loan –, "I begin.

"No. No. I don't ever want to borrow money from family," Martin argues. "We need to create a long-term plan rather than take out loans because we have no idea how long Joshua will continue to need medical help."

His words hang in the air between us. What neither one of us wants to say out loud is that autism is forever.

"We can't simply give up," I cry.

"We aren't giving up. We're simply reconsidering our options," Martin states, then reaches for my hand.

A flood of emotions hit like a tidal wave. I start to sob.

Martin squeezes my hand. "I'm sorry, Abby. Forget I said anything."

Forget? How can I forget something so crucial to my son's well-being? It's like asking me not to breathe. I think about music therapy and how he responds to Ruth – the tug at the corners of his mouth when she sings, or the faint flicker of interest when she hands him the tambourine to shake while she plays a song on the piano. What if he's on the verge of a breakthrough and we rob him of that chance?

I consider aqua therapy and the thrill I experience each time I hold him in my arms. These sessions are the only time Joshua and I connect physically and I need that as much as Joshua needs to learn to swim and trust. There is no way I'll give that up.

There's speech therapy which hasn't yielded much fruit yet, although he's learning the mechanics of sound and dialogue. And occupational therapy, which teaches him sensory processing skills so crucial in rousing his interest. There's Applied Behavior Analysis sessions, the dietary consults, and the monthly visits to the sensory gym where his body and mind are stimulated.

How can I pick what to keep and what to let go? Why should I have to choose in the first place? It's a bit like asking me which body part I can do without. I need each one of them to function properly. Dropping one, let alone several, could be Joshua's undoing.

And my undoing too.

CHAPTER TWENTY-EIGHT

"**N**o, absolutely not!" I cross my arms over my chest, my feet firmly planted. "That dog has been running around the farm, getting into who knows what. She is not sleeping in Joshua's bed tonight."

Martin sighs loudly. "You do realize the doghouse I bought this morning still needs to be assembled?"

"I'll fetch the tools while you read the instructions," I say, marching off to the garage.

Even though I now realize Pooch's germs had nothing to do with Hannah's near-death experience, I'm still not keen on the dog sleeping with Joshua, especially after romping through the fields and chasing chickens.

Thirty minutes later, the doghouse is finally ready. Martin has assembled it in stony silence, the dog watching him with a mixture of interest and wariness.

"Go ahead," I say, pointing to the doghouse. "Try out your new sleeping quarters."

The dog steals a glance at the new structure, then back at me. Obviously, she doesn't trust my intentions.

"It's okay." I infuse a little enthusiasm into my voice, but she's not having it.

Martin yawns loudly. "She might like it better if you put a blanket or something soft inside."

"I don't have any spare blankets," I argue.

Martin shrugs, picks up his tools, and opens the patio door. "You two figure it out, I'm going to bed."

"Come on, girl," I say, patting my leg like Martin.

She plops down on the ground, sighs, then lays her head on her paws like a dejected animal.

"I know you like Joshua's bed, but that's a 'no.' This is where you'll be sleeping from now on," I say, stifling a yawn. "Come on, I'm tired. Let's not take all night about it."

She whines as though I've kicked her to the curb.

"Okay. Fine. Sleep on the lawn if you want. I'm going to bed."

My eyes are like automatic doors on the fritz, shutting, then popping open, over and over again as I undress and hop into the shower. The warm water

186

pelting my shoulders lulls me deeper into a state of lethargy. Cutting my shower short, I turn off the water and wrap myself in an oversized cotton towel.

Out of the darkness rises a deep, blood-curdling howl.

A-roo! A-roo!

A chill runs down my spine. The sound is visceral, soulful, and oh so loud in the somber hours of the night. I pause, listen.

A-roo! A-roo!

Suddenly, I'm wide awake.

A-roo! A-roo!

I shoot a look at the bed. Martin's quiet breathing tells me he's sound asleep. Figures. Quickly donning a pair of pajamas, I bolt down the stairs, snatching an afghan off the back of the sofa as I run by. Yanking the patio doors open, I nearly tread on the dog as I step outside. The furry beast is laying on the bricks, right in front of the doors. She gives me a pitiful look.

"What is wrong with you?" I grumble. "In case you didn't know, people are trying to sleep."

Her tail springs to life, whapping the ground with fervor as I step over her.

"No, I'm not going to let you into the house. You have a nice doghouse all to yourself. Look, I'll even let you borrow one of my afghans to sleep on."

Curious, she follows me and watches, head to the side, as I spread out the blanket inside her kennel.

"There you go. All nice and comfy. Now go to sleep."

Squatting back on my heels, I look at the sky. A star winks in the heavens, as though complicit with my subterfuge. Maybe my little ruse will succeed.

The dog slinks into her kennel, sniffing the blanket and fussing at it with her paws.

"Don't like the way I made your bed? Tough."

With a groan, I push myself to my feet. "Goodnight, you little scoundrel."

I make it all the way back upstairs and into bed, before the howling resumes. I close my eyes, wishing I could shut out the noise. What am I going to do with her? I can't just let her howl. The neighbors will be ringing the cops.

I march back downstairs, yank open the patio doors, and yell, "No!"

For several moments, silence fills the night. Even the cicadas and crickets cease chirping. The dog whimpers and tucks her tail between her legs.

"You're just playing me." I wave a finger at the dog. "I'm fairly certain Brutus, or whatever his name is, didn't allow you to come indoors."

I close my eyes and rub my forehead hoping to ward off another headache. A heavy weight pushes against me and my eyes fly open. The dog presses into my thigh, gazing up at me with doleful eyes. I feel like a heel. This poor dog doesn't deserve my anger. She probably endured enough verbal abuse in her previous home.

"How about a snack? Would that make you happy?"

The dog's tail thumps a brisk tempo.

"Wait here and I'll grab one of those nice, juicy bones Daddy bought for you."

I flinch. Daddy? Seriously?

Stumbling into the kitchen, I pull down the box of dog treats, remove two and take them back outside. The dog barks her pleasure at my return. She's so excited you'd think I'd been gone for several days. With one big pounce, she leaps against me, nearly knocking me over.

"Down!" I say, tossing the treats into the doghouse.

When she darts after them, I scoot back into the house. Anticipating another round of howling, I climb the stairs slowly. But the night is blissfully silent. Slipping into bed, I sigh with pleasure. At last!

I've barely closed my eyes when the howling resumes.

A-roo! A-roo!

I lay there for several minutes, praying she'll settle down on her own. But she won't give up. Tossing back the sheets, I shove my feet into my slippers, then stomp down the hall. As I pass Joshua's room, I hear him stirring. I pause in the doorway. He's wide awake, banging himself in the head with his fist.

"Hey, buddy. You should be asleep," I whisper.

Joshua whines. It sounds eerily similar to the dog's whimpers.

"Are you worried about the dog? She's just saying good night to the moon."

Joshua sits up then hands me his bear Caleb.

"Good night Caleb," I say, giving the bear a kiss on the nose.

Joshua moans when I try to give the bear back to him. He pushes the toy into my chest, then pulls on my arms, wrapping them tightly around the stuffed animal.

"What do you want me to do with Caleb?" I ask, confused.

Joshua pushes me roughly off the bed, the bear still snug in my arms, then glances out the window. It suddenly dawns on me that he wants me to give his bear to the dog.

"Do you want me to give Caleb to the dog so she can snuggle with him?" I ask.

Joshua smiles.

"She will tear it up," I argue.

That's when I realize the dog might be howling because she misses Joshua.

"Why don't I borrow one of your shirts instead? She'll like that because it carries your scent, plus she can lay on it better than a stuffed animal."

He stops hitting himself and allows me to tuck Caleb and him back in bed.

"Good night, Joshua," I whisper, as I cover him with the blankets he's tossed aside.

I pull a shirt he's outgrown out of his dresser drawer, then scurry down the stairs. Outside, the dog continues to howl. If I don't hurry, I'll have the entire neighborhood in an uproar. Sliding open the patio doors, I find the dog sitting in front of her kennel, ears pricked, head slightly cocked. Doesn't she ever sleep?

"Here's one of Joshua's shirts," I say, rubbing it against her snout.

She opens her mouth, snatches it from my hand, then trots off to a dark corner of the yard. I sigh and head back inside just as dirt starts flying. The little stinker is burying my son's shirt!

"Stop!" I screech, stumbling across uneven terrain in the dark. I trip on a tree root, arms flailing as I try to prevent myself from falling nose-first into the dirt. I manage to catch myself, avoiding what could have been a nasty tumble.

In the far corner of the yard, near the fence, the pup is frantically digging, tearing up a section of my lawn with both front paws.

"What are you doing to my lawn?" I grab her collar and drag her away from the hole. "I gave you the shirt to cuddle with, not to bury."

Clutching the shirt in one hand, I use the other to haul her back to the kennel. I toss the shirt in, hoping she'll go in after it. As soon as I let go of her collar, the pup rushes into the doghouse, picks up Joshua's shirt in her mouth, and carries it back to the hole.

"I give up!" I sigh, throwing up my hands. "If you want to dig and that keeps you from howling, then go right ahead. I'm going back to bed."

With a groan of exasperation, I go inside, close the patio doors, then slowly climb the stairs. Somehow, the steps must have multiplied while I was outside. Slipping into bed, I pull the sheets over me and try to relax. But I can't fall asleep. I'm too busy listening to the night.

A-roo! A-roo!

I'm about to elbow Martin awake and make him deal with the dog when the howling stops. I wait, listen, but all is quiet. Puzzled, I lay there for several minutes, muscles taut as I get ready to pounce out of bed. But the howling has finally stopped all on its own.

As I lay there, listening to the silence, my thoughts gradually blur, shutting out the day's worries. I fall asleep.

CHAPTER TWENTY-NINE

The alarm wakes us both 6 a.m. Turning over, I pat Martin's arm.

"Honey, wake up!"

With a grunt, Martin rolls over and slams the snooze button. Sitting on the edge of the bed, he runs a hand through his hair, then pads off to the bathroom. I try to go back to sleep, yet a nagging voice keeps niggling at the dark recesses of my mind. Something feels wrong.

Yawning, I roll onto my back, trying to shut off the alarms going off in my head. The fact that Joshua didn't get up during the night makes me wonder why. Maybe the trip to Grandpa's or the episode with the dog howling have tired him out.

But I don't believe it. Irritated with my overly keen sixth sense, I shove back the sheets, slide both feet into my slippers and stumble down the hall. Just a quick glance into Joshua's room confirms my suspicions; his bed empty, the top sheet pushed aside in a pile.

"Martin!" I yell dashing past our room. I can only hope he hasn't climbed in the shower yet.

Hurtling down the stairs, I run to the front door. I let out the breath I hadn't realized I was holding, relieved to find all three locks still engaged. He hasn't run off. Where is he, then?

My stomach roils. Lurching up the stairs, I race to the bathroom where Martin hums as he showers.

I drop to my knees in front of the toilet and throw up amid strains of "Wide Awake."

Once the vomiting stops, I rock back on my heels.

"Martin!" I yell over the pouring water. "Martin!"

Martin's dripping wet face peers around the shower curtain. "What?" he shouts, then notices me kneeling over the toilet bowl.

"Joshua….," I begin, then lean over the toilet and throw up once more.

Martin's face disappears. Seconds later, the water shuts off and he steps out of the shower.

"I'm sorry you're feeling so poorly," Martin says, grabbing a towel off the rack.

"Don't worry about me," I say, wiping my mouth on a wad of toilet paper. "Joshua's missing."

"Missing?"

"He's not in his bed, not in his room. I don't know where he is."

Like a sprinter out of his block, Martin bolts out of the bathroom. Two seconds later, his face reappears around the door.

"Where have you looked?" His face is etched with worry.

"His room and the front door," I answer, then retch again.

Sitting on the hard, cold bathroom floor, I fight not only the nausea but my own mounting panic. Not again. When will this nightmare ever end?

Downstairs, I hear doors and cupboards slamming as Martin searches the house. Abruptly, the banging ceases. I strain to listen but there's only silence. What happened? Has Martin found Joshua? I push myself off the floor just as Martin strolls into the bathroom. His face is lit up with a smile.

"Did you find him?"

"Yep, I sure did." Martin nods.

"So, where is he?"

"Come see for yourself."

Grabbing a towel off the rack, I stagger down the hall, holding onto the wall for support. Martin grabs my hand to help me down the stairs, then guides me through the living-room to the patio doors.

"This way, please," he says, sliding the doors open and ushering me out to the back yard.

As I step out into the early morning heat, comprehension dawns; Joshua must be in the doghouse. Placing a hand on the kennel roof to steady myself, I lean over and peer inside. Joshua and the dog are sound asleep, curled up together on the afghan.

I glance up at Martin but words fail me.

"Still reluctant to keep the dog?" he asks, one eyebrow raised.

I sigh. There's no denying the powerful bond between these two. Admitting it is a tad bit harder.

"I give!" I say, holding up both hands in mock surrender.

"There is hope for the doubter." Martin laughs, pulling me into a hug. He leans in, resting his forehead against mine. "Thank you."

"You know," I say, looking him in the eyes. "If we're going to keep the dog, we really ought to name her."

"What about Horace?" Martin says.

"That's a terrible name! Besides, that's a boy's name. It needs to be something meaningful, something that describes her relationship with Joshua."

"What about Hope?" Martin says, all humor gone from his voice.

Hope. What a perfect name for the unexpected and uninvited miracle that has stepped into our lives.

"Hope," I whisper. It sounds so right on my tongue. "Hope is definitely the right name for her."

Inside the kennel, soft ruffling noises catch my attention.

"Ope!" A small voice says, from inside the doghouse. It's soft, barely audible, a voice I've never heard before.

I shoot a look at Martin, eyes wide with shock. His hand flies to his mouth as we stare at each other, dumbstruck, knowing we've just witnessed a miracle.

Sinking to my knees, I poke my head inside the doghouse. "What did you say?"

Joshua rubs his eyes and sits up. "Ope," he repeats.

No word has ever sounded so wonderful to a mother's ear.

"You like the name Hope?" I can barely speak for the lump in my throat.

Joshua flings his arms around the puppy's neck. "'Ope."

"Hope! He said hope!" Martin whoops, pumping a fist into the air.

The grin on my face is so wide, it almost hurts. I stand, then wrap my arms around the man who has longed for this day as much as me. Martin hugs me close against his chest. We've both just witnessed a life-changing moment, the budding of that frail seed of hope we've been watching and nurturing for so long.

Hope is, indeed, a fitting name. After all, she's the one who has brought healing to a little boy who, until now, hadn't found his own voice.

EPILOGUE

O NE YEAR LATER

I tie a bright red bandana around the French Poodle's neck and step back to admire my work.

"Bailey looks so pretty, doesn't she?" I say to six-year-old Matthew. He nods, his gaze fixed on the black and white tiled floor.

"Are you ready for your own hair cut now?" I ask, crouching in an effort to lock eyes with him.

The boy doesn't respond. I glance at his mother. She shrugs.

"Come with me, Matthew." I hold out my hand, surprised when the boy takes it.

Simon is waiting for us at the cutting station. "Wow! Abby did a great job with Bailey, didn't she Matthew?" he says.

The boy nods, without making eye contact. Hesitant, Matthew looks at the barber chair.

"This chair is special. It goes up and down and spins around."

The boy casts a quick glance at the barber chair but won't climb into it. I sense he's afraid.

"Remember when you helped me trim Bailey's fur?"

Matthew nods.

"It didn't hurt at all, did it?"

He looks at Bailey who's laying on the floor, tongue lolling out the side of her mouth.

"Bailey was very brave when we washed her and trimmed her fur. Now it's your turn to be brave while Bailey watches you get your hair trimmed." I deliberately avoid the term "cut" as it often conveys a notion of pain.

Slowly, Matthew steps onto the footrest then climbs into the chair.

"Good job!" I say, smiling at the boy. "When you're done, Simon will let you choose a prize from his treasure box."

I smile at Simon, then quietly scoot back to my own salon named Snip 'n Clip. A few months ago, I purchased the wool shop that was going out of business, the one right next door to Doo or Dye Hair Salon. A contractor was able to fashion an archway in the wall connecting the two spaces, creating an easy transition from one salon to the other. Although open to the public in general, Snip 'n Clip is geared towards individuals with special-needs. When owners bring their dogs to my pet-grooming salon, they are invited to assist, if they so wish. This hands-on approach helps individuals with autism and other special needs to grasp the washing, drying, clipping, and grooming process which helps alleviate some of their own fears and apprehensions about having their hair cut.

Grabbing a broom, I sweep Bailey's clippings into a pile, then brush them into the dustpan. As I dump the fur into the trashcan, the bell above the shop door tinkles. Becky's smiling face peers around the door.

"Becky!" I squeal, rushing to help her into the store.

My daughter Grace is asleep in the kangaroo pouch strapped to my sister's chest while Becky's daughter, Julie, rides in the stroller. Bringing up the rear are Joshua and Hope. Joshua is tethered to Hope, preventing him from dashing off or running into traffic.

Joshua's face breaks into a big smile as he enters the shop. My heart skips a beat for sheer joy. I love this boy so much it hurts.

"Did you have fun at the park with Aunt Becky?" I ask, crouching to his level.

He nods. "Ice-cweam," he says, casting a quick glance my way before averting his eyes.

"She bought you ice-cream?" I ask, reaching to give him a light hug. He doesn't pull away from me as much anymore, as long as I don't squeeze too hard or hold him too long.

"'nilla," he says.

"Vanilla? Yum." I glance up at Becky who's visiting for a few days. "Did he do okay?"

"He was fine. Grace, too. She slept most of the time. Julie was the fussy one."

Julie is a beautiful little girl, with long, raven-colored hair. She looks just like my sister Becky when she was little. Grace, our precious four-month-old daughter, is sound asleep, a trickle of drool dangling from the corner of her mouth. So far, she hasn't shown any signs of autism. In fact, she's the most contented child I've ever known.

"Is Ginger coming to relieve you soon?" Becky asks.

I glance at my watch. "Should be here any minute."

Ginger is the young woman I met at the drugstore several months ago, when I stopped to buy hair dye. She works for me part-time now which helps a lot seeing as business is booming. I know the shop is in good hands when she's here which allows me to divide my time between work and my two little ones.

Ginger is wonderful with the customers and understands their unique issues. In fact, she's taking classes at Missouri State University towards a degree in psychology. She wants to work full-time with individuals on the autism spectrum.

"Here, let me help you put the kids in the car," I say, grabbing Julie's stroller.

Hope and Joshua follow me out the door. True to his word, Martin took Hope for training. Not merely for behavior, but to become Joshua's Autism Service Dog. After several weeks, Hope officially received her certification, which allows Joshua to take her everywhere with him.

Joshua has slowly found his voice. With help from a speech therapist, he will eventually catch up with his peers. Thanks to Hope, his meltdowns are less frequent and less intense. She helps him refocus when he grows anxious and her presence offers the comfort he so desperately needs. Joshua even allows me to hold his hand upon occasion. We are making progress and that's all I've ever asked for.

Hope has come in her own, gentle way, changing our lives forever. Hope, not only for Joshua but for our entire family.

AUTHOR'S NOTE

Although this story is fiction, it is based upon countless true stories of individuals with autism, who found their voices with the help of dogs. There are numerous groups that offer Autism Service Dogs, specially trained to provide assistance, emotional support, and safety. These dogs are taught to recognize the onset of a meltdown and help de-escalate and interrupt self-harming behaviors.

To find out more about autism service dogs, check sites such as Dog's Nation, Autism Service Dogs of America, 4 Paws For Ability, Pawsitivity Service Dogs, Paws with a Cause, or Canines 4 Hope.

Born to an American father and a British mother, Renée Vajko Srch grew up in France where she obtained her French Baccalaureate. She attended IBME in Switzerland, graduating with a degree in Theology. She is a speaker with Stars for Autism, educating and training individuals and businesses about autism.

She currently lives in the Missouri Ozarks with her husband and three sons, one of whom has been diagnosed with Asperger's. She is a connoisseur of fine chocolates, loves to read, and has a weakness for rescue cats.

She is a staff-writer for Herald and Banner Press. Several of her articles have been published in the Missouri Autism Report magazine. Two of her stories have been published in *Chicken Soup for the Soul* books. She also authors a blog on autism, motherhood and God. She is currently working on her second novel, ghostwriting a memoir, and a devotional for autism and special-needs families.

You can follow her on Facebook (Author Renée Vajko Srch), Twitter (Renee Srch@SrchRenee), Pinterest (MotherhoodAutismAndGod), and Instagram (ReneeVajkoSrch). She blogs at www.MotherhoodAutismAndGod.blogspot.com